Shakey's Madness

Shakey's Madness

Does a Mental Disorder Reveal the "Real" William Shakespeare?

Robert Boog

ths international publishing

CONTENTS

DEDICATION

This book is dedicated to my beautiful wife Roxana Boog and our two sons, Brandon and Kevin.

Always know that you are in my heart and I am very proud of you.

1

Preface

At my house, my main job besides feeding the dogs, and picking up the dog poop, involves taking out the trash. Come Friday, I wheel three large trash bins out to the street.

We have lived at the same house for over 20 years, and the trash truck comes on Friday morning. I had a perfect record of taking the bins to the curb -- until a couple of months ago, when I slipped up.

I forgot to bring the bins out to the street! No biggie, right?

But then the following week, I forgot again!

My wife did not find it amusing. “Robert,” she said, “This cannot happen again. In fact, next week, you had better bring those bins out to the street by Thursday evening. Or else.” Then she stomped off leaving me to wonder what “or else” meant.

Fast forward to the following week.

Thursday evening found me wheeling the trash bins to the street when I caught a glimpse of my next-door neighbor doing the same thing. He took one look at me and started to laugh. He said, “Dang, dude. You sure have a lot of trash!”

I said, “Yeah man, well, what about you?”

“Nah, we hardly have anything,” he said. “See, we have been on vacation for the past two weeks.”

Then it dawned on me.

I had been stealing my neighbor's cue. Seeing his trash cans parked out on the curb was what had reminded me to bring out our trash cans.

Similarly, when it comes to the authorship of William Shakespeare, most of us have a comparable blind allegiance.

We have been taught that William Shakespeare wrote the poems, plays, and sonnets attributed to him. So, why should we doubt it? In fact, if you do question it, some folks will say, "You must be crazy, because no legitimate scholar questions his authorship."

You might even be labeled a "flat earth believer," "a crank," or a "conspiracy theorist" and who wants that? But thousands of intelligent people HAVE doubted the Bard's authorship.

Famous people too, like Sigmund Freud. Henry James. Malcolm X, Charlie Chaplin, and Mark Twain. It has been going on for a long time!

So, why doubt Shakespeare?

You will find out in a minute, and I am going to offer you my own original opinion.

Remember, the Webster-Meriam dictionary defines "an opinion" as "a generally held belief" that "implies a conclusion thought out yet open to dispute." You can freely agree, disagree, or come up with your own hypothesis.

But, after reading this book, hopefully you will decide to fact-check me at the library, Google, Bing, YouTube or wherever you do your research.

My experience? I graduated from UCLA with a BA in British Literature. I enjoy the works attributed to William Shakespeare. In fact, so much, I rewrote one of his sonnets (my instructor's favorite). You will find my masterpiece in this book too.

My instructor did say, "We know more about the life of Jesus Christ than we do of William Shakespeare," and for some reason that remark stuck with me. But to be honest, for about 35 years I did not think that much about Shakespeare because I attended graduate school at the college of hard knocks.

I work in the highly competitive field of Los Angeles real estate.

Listing homes, flipping homes, staging homes, selling homes, and condos? You name it. I have done it. I have listed and sold everything from vacant land to million-dollar mansions.

In other words, I come from the world where all buyers are liars, agents cannot be trusted, and sellers often do not tell the truth.

One time, for example, the seller of a vacant parcel of land told me that his property featured a water well that pumped 7.5 gallons per minute. He even emailed me a document from a water well company to prove it.

This convinced my buyer to want to submit a full-price bid because to build a new home on vacant land, the Los Angeles County Building and Safety Department requires that a water well pumps at a minimum of 7.5 gallons per minute.

To verify, I called the company that had drilled the well and spoke to the well-driller who told me, "If it says 7.5 gallons per minute on the document then why don't you believe it?"

I said, "I am sorry sir, but could I just email you this document? I am just not familiar with these things."

After reviewing the document, he called me and said, "You have a well-share agreement for three vacant parcels of land. The well currently pumps water at 7.5 gallons per minute- allowable for one house, but not for any additional homes."

After relaying his words to the buyers, we moved on and, I helped them purchase a different property.

Want to know one thing I have found after dealing with sharks and very smart people? Do NOT accept something to be true just because someone tells you it is true.

You must think like a detective, investigate things, and then double-check them.

Like the TV detective, Mr. Monk.

2

Introducing Mr. Monk

I have a confession to make. I am a Monkaholic. One of my favorite TV detective programs is *Monk* and I have watched every single episode.

The show features Tony Shalhoub who portrays a quirky, former police detective named Adrian Monk who has OCD (obsessive-compulsive disorder) and a wide variety of phobias which often help him to solve complex crimes.

In the episode, *Mr. Monk Bumps His Head*, for example, a case of amnesia helps Monk to rediscover his weaknesses and strengths.

For Monkaholics like me, watching Monk figuring things out in a brand-new environment makes me smile. He has over three hundred phobias including fears of milk, heights, and things out of balance. So, with his amnesia, when Monk truly believes a woman who claims him as her husband, it is almost cringeworthy to see him do things that would normally appall him.

But, hearing Monk talk about how he truly feels about himself, others, and his life makes one consider the life of William Shakespeare.

What challenges and setbacks in his life did he have? How did he handle them? Why don't we know anything about him?

Most of us have been taught that writers should "write about what they know" but, if William Shakespeare hailed from Stratford-upon-

Avon, and was a "commoner," why did he not write about, commonplace stuff?

Why did he fill his plays with foreign places like Italy and Greece? Why feature nobles, aristocratic pursuits, and things an ordinary person would know *nothing* about? In the *Merchant of Venice*, for example, Shylock talks about meeting at "the Rialto" which was a bridge. It would not show up on any maps.

How would someone who never left England know about it?

Yet playbills, the book of Sonnets and the First Folio which contains a collection of Shakespeare's thirty-six plays identify William Shakespeare as the author of the Shakespeare canon. Experts repeatedly tell us there is no direct evidence to prove that anyone other than William Shakespeare was the author of the Shakespeare canon.

Thankfully, lack of direct evidence has not stopped prosecutors from winning court cases involving serial killers.

Or should we just leave well enough alone? After all, no one has doubted Shakespeare's authorship in over 300 years. Does it even matter?

What would Mr. Monk say?

3

Why Doubt Shakespeare's Authorship?

You might be thinking, "Who cares whether or not William Shakespeare wrote the works attributed to him?" And I get it because many people have felt this way. After all, over 400 years have passed and there is no direct proof existing for any other candidate. But what we have found is just like there is no statute of limitations for murder, why not look at this like a cold case mystery? One where clues have been left behind for armchair detectives like you and me and Mr. Monk.

Then again, maybe I am getting ahead of myself, because in most episodes of Monk, don't viewers get to see some kind of back story? So, let us back up a bit, shall we?

A Royal Serial Killer?

Did you know that King Henry VIII married six times and beheaded two of his wives because they failed to produce a male heir? It's true. Then, after Henry passed away, his son, King Edward VI died at age 15 after holding the throne for six years. Next came, England's first true female monarch, Queen "Bloody" Mary, and finally Queen Elizabeth I who ruled England for over 44 years.

Queen Elizabeth I

So, Queen Elizabeth I *was the daughter* of King Henry VIII the man who had beheaded two of his wives. Elizabeth has been called the "Virgin Queen" because she never married, but the word "virgin" somehow implies innocence and chasteness. Was she a flawless woman who was as pure as the driven snow?

No. Elizabeth was brutally cunning and could be as fickle, ferocious, and ruthless as her father. Fiercely Protestant, during her reign, 125 Roman Catholic priests met a violent end -- disemboweled before they met their maker. Why? Because the priests had heard the confessions of their parishioners. To Catholics, confession might have been a sacred act, but Queen Elizabeth considered it an "act of treason".

Here is another fun fact: a royal edict from around 1350 stated that any British citizen of the realm could be charged with high treason for such slight infractions as:

- Stating the sovereign was a tyrant.
- Ridiculing the ruler.
- "Imagining the death" of a Queen or King.

Living in such treacherous times, when making fun of a ruler could be punishable by being gutted in public, followed by death, why would anyone in his right mind pen a drama that someone else might interpret as "imagining the death of the ruler?"

Royals, noblemen and noblewomen dominate Shakespeare's works. Thirty-four plays in the First Folio present the Ruler, Prince, or Monarch of the state where the events take place and *Hamlet, Cleopatra, Richard II*, and *Henry V* all feature rulers who die. (The chorus lets us know Henry dies.) Cleopatra kills herself. Hamlet, who is a prince, dies of poisoning but not before he kills Claudius, the king of Denmark.

In 1601, an aged Queen Elizabeth I (she passed away in 1603) watched a performance of the play *Richard II* which included a scene where the king resigns his throne.

Since she had not named a successor, what was Queen Elizabeth's reaction to the play?

Shakespeare experts tell us the coronation of a King or Queen is not supposed to be undone, and in the play, Bolingbroke's insistence that Richard voluntarily give up his crown in front of witnesses shows his understanding that **the putting on and taking off of crowns needs to be public to be meaningful**. It also turned the peasants' rebellion into a civilized ceremony.

Imagine the scene. When the Queen arrived, everyone there would be obliged to rise. When she sat down, everyone followed. Next, The Lord Chamberlain's players performed *Richard II* and featured William Shakespeare as both actor and playwright.

Shakespeare expert, Sir Stanley Wells tells us that the Queen "most likely" had met Shakespeare many times because he had performed many of his plays before her at court. So, what was Queen Elizabeth's reaction after she viewed *Richard II*? We know she told several people later, "Don't you get it? I am Richard II."

She reacted swiftly, unexpectedly and violently. Sir Gelly Meyrick who had paid for the performance was immediately hung, drawn, and quartered. This means before he died from hanging, his intestines were yanked out first, then burned, and then four horses snapped his bloody body apart. Can you imagine the horrid sight, sounds, and smells?

Robert Devieriex

Next, Robert Devereux, the earl of Essex, was tried in a court of law, found guilty of treason, and beheaded. Written accounts claim it took three whacks of the executioner's ax to sever his head from his bleeding neck.

Some people will yawn and claim this was part of the Essex Rebellion where Robert Devereux led one hundred of his men into London to enlist the peasants to rebel against the queen. Unlike the play *Richard II*, however, no angry peasant crowds were found in London, so Devereux's men deserted him. The two leaders, Robert Devereux and Henry Wriothesley were arrested. What happened to Henry Wriothesley?

Henry received life imprisonment in the Tower of London. (His sentence was later commuted by King James I.) And William Shakespeare? Was he hunted down, maimed and executed?

No.

William Shakespeare was NOT even questioned. This seems odd because in 1593 and 1594, Shakespeare had allegedly dedicated two long poems to Henry Wriothesley. Plus, didn't Shakespeare write *Richard II*? When citing "contemporary sources", experts point to Shakespeare's name being found on the title page of *Richard II*.

My point is, Shakespeare, Devereux and Henry Wriothesley all acted as co-conspirators, did they not? Why was Shakespeare not even questioned?

Answer: the queen *must have known* William Shakespeare was **not** the author of the play. If so, she would have had his head.

But what if Queen Elizabeth respected William Shakespeare and feared a rebellion if she killed him? Ha ha. The queen ruled by fear and would execute anyone. She risked a war with Spain by decapitating her stepsister, Mary Queen of Scots and she had done it anyway. Elizabeth liked Robert Devereux, her cousin because she often danced with him, but any person who dared to challenge the queen's authority would be put to death. Therefore, the queen's lack of action with the Bard tells us that **someone else** must have written *Richard II*.

If Shakespeare the vagabond actor did not write it, then he did not write any other play attributed to him too.

But if William Shakespeare was NOT the author of the plays attributed to him, then who was?

In this book, I will prove that circumstantial evidence points to only one person: Edward de Vere, the seventeenth earl of Oxford.

Edward de Vere left his fingerprints throughout the works that have all been attributed to William Shakespeare.

Please be aware that in these pages, I am trying to avoid using footnotes. My tone will be more conversational than a history book and I may even slip in some personal stories and humor. I want to inspire you to investigate the Shakespeare authorship mystery on your own. Who knows? You may find data that I have missed.

What is Circumstantial Evidence?

Many court cases nowadays are won because of circumstantial evidence, which is defined as "evidence that relies on **an inference** to connect it to a conclusion of fact." Most Shakespeare scholars would have people believe that direct evidence is better than circumstantial evidence but this is not true. Circumstantial evidence is often MORE important than direct evidence.

For example, DNA evidence or a fingerprint left at the scene of a crime infers that the perpetrator must have been there. This is a good example of circumstantial evidence. There is little doubt about the perpetrator being there while an example of direct evidence can be an eyewitness who claims he or she saw the defendant at the crime scene.

Direct evidence is not always reliable because a person could have bad vision or a faulty memory.

So, what evidence proves de Vere wrote the works?

We will visit this topic in future chapters but first, here are three questions that may raise doubts about William Shakespeare's authorship.

QUESTION#1: Why Toss Shakespeare's Letters? For over 20 years, William Shakespeare worked in London, about one hundred miles away from his family in Stratford-upon-Avon. Back then, it was a 2–3-day journey by horse to get to London, so writing a letter made sense. Experts also claim Shakespeare collaborated with other writers. Yet not one letter either "to" or "from" William Shakespeare has ever been discovered in over 400+ years. Would you have kept a letter written to you by William Shakespeare? If he didn't write any letters, why not?

QUESTION #2: Why Illiterate Family Members? William Shakespeare's father and mother were both illiterate, so they did NOT read books to him. His wife Anne and daughter Judith both signed their names with a mark, so they could not read or write.

William's oldest daughter Susanna could sign her name, so if William had written a letter to his wife, his oldest daughter might have read it. The plays and poems are full of classical illusions meaning that he read widely.

But it seems odd or cruelly sexist that the world's greatest writer did not care that his two daughters could ever read.

QUESTION #3: Why Retire from the Arts? Many movie or TV actors will proclaim: "One does not get into the theater--the theater gets into you." Plenty of people dream of leaving their 9-5 jobs to work in show business. But William Shakespeare? He retired early from the arts to pursue his true passion in life: lending money. Weird.

As I mentioned earlier, Detective Adrian Monk has obsessive-compulsive disorder and a keen eye for detail. In every episode of Monk, the observant detective notices tiny circumstantial details that others easily miss, and only by zeroing in and fitting the pieces together can Monk finally solve the crime.

Adrian Monk often appraises a crime scene with his two hands forming an imaginary video screen so he can imagine what really happened. In fact, his catchphrase is "Here's what happened."

In the next chapter, we will view some circumstantial evidence regarding William Shakespeare's youth.

It shows William Shakespeare's original baptized name was NOT William Shakespeare.

4

Guilielmus Who?

People nowadays call him William, but did you know that William Shakespeare's baptismal name was Guilielmus Shaksper? You can see it for yourself by checking his baptismal record found online at the Folger Website. Here we see his name registered as: Guilielmus filius Johannes Shaksper, and there are three X's to the right of it. Only one "e" was in his last name: Shaksper.

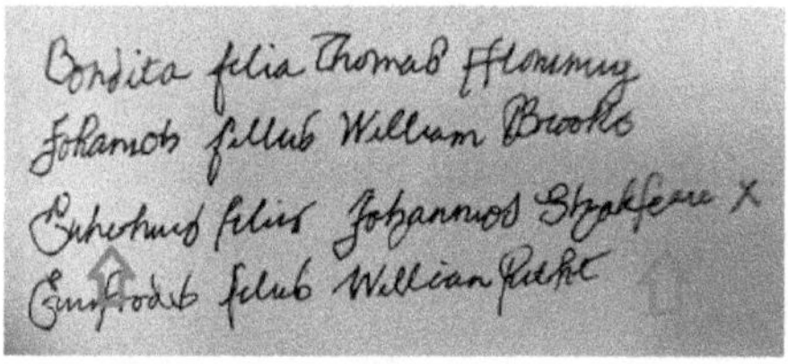

Reproduction. Actual image at the Folger Shakespeare Library

Most scholars will say "no worries." Guilielmus filius Johannes Shaksper means "William, son of John Shaksper"in Latin. This might be true. Guilielmus can mean William, but people still use this name today and will pronounce it "Gilly- el-mus." (Like when David Bowie sings, "Jamming good with Weird and Gilly and the Spiders from

Mars.") You can put the name "Guilielmus" into Google to hear it for yourself.

If John Shaksper had wanted his son to be called William, why not call him Willelmus? Or John could have simply said "William" and the scribe would have printed that name. But he did not. The person above and below Guilielmus Shakesper did this, and we can see the name William written above and below Guilielmus with our own eyes.

So, maybe John did not want his son to be named William. Perhaps he thought "Willy" might be teased. Might they say, "Willy shakes his spear?" It makes sense, does it not?

This may seem trivial, but William Shakespeare of Stratford-upon-Avon started out as someone born to parents who both signed their names with a mark. He did not grow up listening to stories read to him by his parents because they could not read.

What about his Grammar School Education?

Legend has it that William Shakespeare lived in Stratford-upon-Avon and attended the King Edward VI grammar school. The Folger Library contains **the world's largest Shakespeare collection and is the ultimate resource for exploring Shakespeare and his world.** Their website tells us: "Shakespeare, as the son of a leading Stratford citizen, **almost certainly** attended Stratford's grammar school. Like all such schools, its curriculum consisted of an intense emphasis on the Latin classics, including memorization, writing, and acting classic Latin plays. Shakespeare **most likely** attended until about age 15."

Notice the wiggle room? The Folger writes "almost certainly" and "most likely" because no records exist of Stratford ever attending any school. So, academics have worked the equation backward. Because Stratford's name can be found on the title of the First Folio, he "must have" attended school.

The Folger also tells us that as an "alderman" or mayor of the town, William's father, John Shakespeare would have been entitled to give his son a "free" education.

Stratfordians (people who hold that it was Shakespeare who wrote the plays of William Shakespeare) further tell us that grammar schools back in the Elizabethan times were extremely strict. They mostly focused on teaching Latin.

Do we have proof William Shakespeare ever attended any school much less a grammar school?

No. None whatsoever.

The only proof of being home-schooled like an apprentice is the fact that his father liked to lend money and so did William. The math for lending money is algebra which would not be taught at a grammar school.

Therefore, people who support William Shakespeare as the author of Shakespeare will often ask "are not some geniuses self-taught?" Or "do not some people learn things after the leave school?" Or even "why is it important that a poetic genius attend school at all?"

Why was a grammar school education important for William Shakespeare to be considered the "real" author?

5

A Grammar School Education?

Stratfordian scholars tell us a school day back in Shakespeare's time began at 7:00 am and lasted until 6:00 pm for six days a week. William "most likely" started his education at age seven and ended it at age 15. This is important because as you will soon see, the "real" author had to be an expert in Latin which was taught mainly at grammar schools. But did you know that circumstantial evidence found online offers a much different story about Will's grammar school education?

First a little backstory. During the Elizabethan era, most Catholics did NOT believe that children needed to attend school: only the ones who were going to be Bishops or Priests.

Why? Because **only** Priests and Bishops needed to know how to read and interpret the Bible. Then too, there were also parents who were not Catholic who held a sexist belief that school was not meant for girls.

So out of a town populated with 1,350 people there may have been 135 children and if 20% attended classes how many students might be in the entire school? 135 x 20% = **27.**

Also, most experts tell us that girls did NOT attend school, but we have evidence that contradicts this: the 1598 court testimony of Elizabeth Evans and Joice Cowden.

Elizabeth Evans, who lived in London signed her name in a nice italic script. Accused of being a prostitute, Evans testified in court that she had grown up in Stratford-upon-Avon. Because Elizabeth had used several pen names, Joice Cowden was called to testify to the identity of Elizabeth Evans since they had both grown up in the same town.

Cowden testified that "she doth knowe Elizabeth Evans and further saith that they went to the same school together in Stratford-upon-Avon."

However, Cowden signed her name with a mark, even though she admitted in court that she had gone to school in Stratford-upon-Avon. (Feel free to Google Joice Cowden!)

Was there more than one school in Stratford-upon-Avon? No, only one school existed in the town of Stratford-upon-Avon but at that time, most children were home-schooled. This means a student would serve as an apprentice where they would learn the math of a carpenter, for example, directly from a carpenter.

But, if William Shakespeare had attended school in Stratford-upon-Avon would it be the top-notch, six-days a week grammar school that modern scholars might have you believe? No.

John Shakespeare and his wife were both raised as Catholics so it would be more likely for their second son, Gilbert, to attend school. The oldest son, William, would inherit their property and Gilbert would be next in line or become a priest. Compare Gilbert Shakespeare's signature to his brother William's. By the way, Gilbert Shakespeare never married.

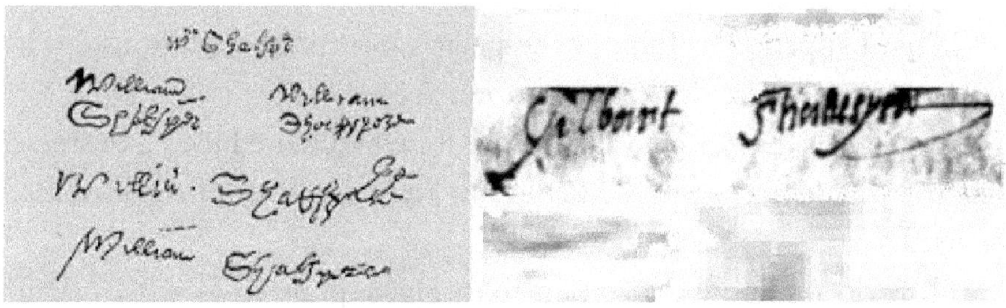

Images courtesy of Google images.

For those keeping score, I am using Google images to make it easier to verify the information in this book. The images are mostly over 400 years old or free images.

Back to the signatures: does this comparison really prove anything circumstantially? Not yet, so let us continue.

We have been told that William Shakespeare was born in 1564 and attended grammar school from age 7 to 15. This means he would have started school in 1571 and ended school in 1579.

But what if his father John Shakespeare did NOT live in the town of Stratford-upon-Avon during this time? How would William attend school?

I mention this because two documents found at the Folger library claim John Shakespeare was a tenant. The transaction concerns a property sale by a Mr. William Clopton and Mr. William Sheldon to Mr. Edmund Griffin and Mr. Rice Griffin.

I want you to remember the name **Rice Griffin**.

These two documents list John Shakespeare as a tenant of a 121-acre farm located in Ingon Meadow which is about five miles away from Stratford-upon-Avon and the birthplace trust home. Other tenants included John Combe, Ralph Cawdrey, Roger Sadler, and Lewis Ap Williams who all show up in the town ledgers. Like John Shakespeare, they acted as an "alderman" and other positions on the Stratford town council.

What happened to John Shakespeare's birthplace trust house? The one on Henley Street in Stratford-upon-Avon?

Most likely, John leased it out, and if he had rented it to a business, like the Maidenhead Inn, he could not return to it until the lease had expired.

How do we know for certain John Shakespeare lived at this farm? The Folger library has copies of the original real estate sales documents. You can see them for yourself online. They (not me) show a date of

1570 and William Shakespeare may have been living on this farm until 1578. Living five miles away, do you really think William would still attend the King Edward VI grammar school?

See for yourself. Can you make out John Shakespeare's name on or about the third line down the middle?

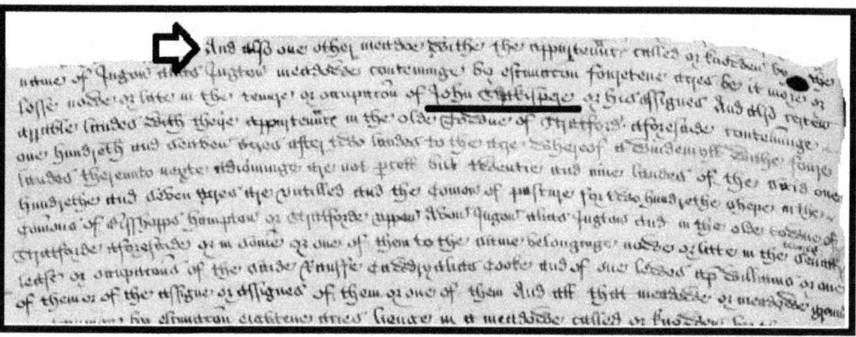

Above image is from https://shakespearedocumented.folger.edu/

The text at the arrow reads: "and also one other meadow along with its appurtenances, called or known by the name of Ingon, alias Ington Meadow, containing by **estimation fourteen acres** be it more or less, now or late in the tenure or occupation of **John Shakespeare** or his assigns, **and also** the arable lands along with their appurtenance in the old town of Stratford aforesaid containing **one hundred and seven acres**, after two hands to the acre, whereof a **windmill.**"

(Translation courtesy of Nina Green.)

John Shakespeare's lease entitled him to a total of 121 acres (14 plus 107 acres =121 acres) plus a windmill!

Has any teacher ever told you that William Shakespeare grew up on a farm with a windmill?

No. I did not think so. See? They were holding out on us!

One hundred twenty-one acres seems like a lot of land and having a windmill might mean William Shakespeare could have been busy putting grain in sacks for other farmers instead of attending school.

John Shakespeare may have even had to pay more money to the Queen in taxes because of this windmill.

Some people will see "John Shakespeare or his assigns" and say, "Aha. The word "assigns" in real estate means "to transfer." Perhaps John transferred this property to his brother Henry Shakespeare who lived nearby. This would allow John to live in town while Henry farmed there, would it not? Here are four reasons why this does not make sense:

1. **John's Property Owner was Selling.** In 1570, John's proprietor, William Clopton was selling the property to Rice Griffin and his brother Edmund Griffin. The contract had to be approved by Queen Elizabeth and if it were not true, Clopton would be in big trouble. Today, a seller could be sued for fraud or breach of contract if a tenant sublet a property without the landlord's consent. In those days, Clopton might have been hung for fraud and misrepresentation. To transfer the property, John would have had to surrender the property first and no longer be a tenant. The transition would be recorded in the rolls of the court with a copy handed to the owner. This did not happen.
2. **Henry Higford**. If John Shakespeare had transferred occupancy of the farm to his brother, and did live in town, then why can't Henry Higford find John Shakespeare? Henry Higford was the former lawyer for the Stratford Corporation and personally knew John Shakespeare. The two had worked together. Higford could recognize him on sight.

Records show that Higford went to Stratford-upon-Avon in 1573 and 1578 to serve John with a lawsuit. So, why can't Henry Higford find John Shakespeare?

One entry at the Shakespeare Documented website reads: **Court of Common Pleas, Plea Roll; action by Henry Higford against John Shakespeare and John Musshem for debt, 15 Eliz I Easter**.

1. **John Needed Space for his Wool**. According to the Folger, during the 1570's, John made massive wool purchases. He purchased two hundred tods of wool in 1571, or 5,600 lbs. of wool. If John Shakespeare lived in town, where would John store all this wool? Purchasing this much wool to resell without a license was illegal. Wouldn't the neighbors talk? If we do the math John Shakespeare had about $80,000 invested in this deal. Common sense tells us if you invested $80,000 in buying illegal weed or wool, or something desirable that someone else might want to steal, would you live several miles away from the goods? Or close to it?
2. **John Shakespeare Called Himself a "Yeoman".** The Folger tells us that when William Shakespeare was eleven, John Shakespeare no longer called himself a "glover" which involved butchering, tanning hides, and making gloves. (Most work gloves were made of leather.) What occupation did John claim in official written legal documents? A yeoman. John lists himself as a "yeoman" or farmer (a step down from a gentleman but a step above a husbandman) when he acted as a witness on a deed in 1575. This deed was for a neighbor selling his property on Henley Street. Now, John may have called himself a yeoman to sound more like a big shot, but who knows? A farmer fits in better living on a 121-acre property at Ingon Meadow, doesn't it?

Does any of this stop William Shakespeare from walking five miles to the grammar school to receive a free education? No. But it seems unlikely. Today, most of us can walk five miles in one hour. Back then it took a man five days to walk 100 miles, so there may have been thicker forests. If it took a grown man 2.5 hours to walk five miles, how long might it take a child to hoof it five miles to school? It does not mean that he couldn't do it, it just seems highly unlikely.

It also makes it less believable for William Shakespeare to have read the books he needed to read to be the real author.

The British Library, for example, claims the Bard read two versions of Ovid's 15 book masterpiece, *Metamorphosis*. One version in English, translated by Arthur Golding and the other in Latin. The British Library states:

"William Shakespeare knew of Golding's Ovid and recalls it in several of his plays. However, Shakespeare did have knowledge of versions other than Golding's—for instance, a passage in Shakespeare's The Tempest seems to have a closer resemblance to the original Latin text than to Golding's English version. "

John Purchases Two Messuages in 1575

On October 22, 1575, John Shakespeare purchased two "messuages" from Edmund Hall located in the town of Stratford-upon-Avon. Many people interpret "messuages" to mean buildable lots while others claim a messuage can also mean a lot with a house on it. The Folger account reads: "two messuages, two gardens and two orchards." Therefore, could not John have moved back to town in October of 1575? Yes.

So, could not William Shakespeare have started school then? It is possible, but how long was a school year? The school year for Abe Lincoln in 1809 in a similar farming region ended before the harvest. So, if William had moved to town in October of 1575, would he have attended school that year? It's doubtful.

Also, experts tell us that Shakespeare left school in 1578, so would he really possess *an extensive* knowledge of Greek and Latin? No. Remember Joice Cowden signed her name with a mark.

Is there circumstantial evidence proving William left school early? Yes. The author E.K. Chambers who in 1930 wrote *William Shakespeare: A Study of Facts and Problems* includes an account by a man named Nicholas Rowe who in 1709, stated:

"His father bred him at a free school but withdrew him owing to the narrowness of his circumstances, and the want of his assistance at home."

John Shakespeare had a wife plus seven more mouths to feed. Certainly, he may have wanted William to attend school, but might John have needed the money?

A son under the legal age was obligated to give any earnings to his father, so perhaps William went to work at Richard Hathaway's farm and that is how he fell for Anne Hathaway. Is this also how William Shakespeare met the two guarantors for his marriage bond, Fulke Sandels and John Richardson?

Do These Thoughts Resonate?

1. Scholars claim without any proof that William Shakespeare attended grammar school in town, but online documents tell a different story.
2. They show that his father was a tenant of a 121-acre farm located five miles out of town.
3. Experts also tell us William Shakespeare "must have" read two versions of a 15-book poem, one version in English, and one in Latin.

But how could he have read fifteen books in Latin if his father had taken him out of school early, due to "the narrowness of his circumstances?" If William did not attend school, where would he find books? Taking them? Stealing something as trivial as eggs could result in hanging. Also, William's father had a tough time financially, and as a result he was shunned by townspeople. So, there was nobody gifting books in Greek or Latin to young William so he could write a Greek play like *Timon of Athens.*

Athens is in Greece, isn't it?

Also, there were no public lending libraries. Therefore, a lack of books and not having an extensive education makes it unlikely that William of Stratford would have had the learning necessary to produce the works attributed to him.

For this reason, Stratford scholars will dig their heels in the ground and die on that hill, insisting that John Shakespeare would **never** live on a farm at Ingon Meadow.

They say this even though in 1602, William Shakespeare purchased 107 acres from his father's old neighbor, John A. Combe for the sum of £320.

Question: From whom had John A. Combe purchased the property he then flipped to William Shakespeare?

Answer: **Rice Griffin**. Remember him?

6

Who was Oxford?

People who believe that Edward de Vere, the 17th earl of Oxford aka "Oxford" was the person who wrote the works of William Shakespeare are called "Oxfordians".

The man responsible for first suggesting Edward de Vere was really Shakespeare was a British school teacher by the name of J. Thomas Looney (pronounced Lou-knee).

Back in 1920, Looney found himself puzzled by the details of Italy found in the Shakespeare works. He knew that the Bard had never traveled outside of England.

J. Thomas Looney

From the records Looney researched, William Shakespeare was portrayed as a shrewd and frugal property owner. However, the man who had authored the plays was a reckless spender who thought of material objects as trifles.

Shakespeare also possessed expert legal knowledge which also puzzled him, as most commoners at that time were not so conversant with the law. Plus, no records showed that William Shakespeare had taken the time to study it.

Looney's book was titled *Shakespeare Identified in Edward de Vere the Seventeenth Earl of Oxford* so: Who was Oxford?

Before I get into talking about Edward de Vere or "Oxford" a documentary film, *Nothing is Truer than True*, tells de Vere's story visually. It got me started out on my authorship quest and I highly recommend that anyone, especially students watch it.

Edward de Vere

Edward de Vere the 17th earl of Oxford (scholars have nicknamed him "Oxford") was born in 1550. His father served on the Royal Court of Queen Mary Tudor (Bloody Mary). Because his father feared for his son's safety, he and his wife allowed Edward to be raised at the home of Sir Thomas Smith, an author and former Cambridge and Greek scholar.

Thomas Smith and his wife were childless. From Smith, Oxford first learned Greek and then Latin along with languages such as French, Italian, and Spanish. Smith also taught young Edward higher mathematics, astronomy, religion, and music.

At the tender age of eight, Oxford visited Queen's College, Cambridge, and records show that a "Viscount Edward Bulbeck" (Oxford held several ancestral titles) attended Cambridge in the autumn term of 1558. Oxford's wealthy parents owned Hedingham Castle.

His father also maintained a company of players called Lord Oxford's Men, who performed plays four times a year. When Edward could go home to visit his parents, his father taught him shooting, horsemanship, falconry, and other aristocratic society pursuits. These activities show up in Shakespeare's plays.

During his visits to Hedingham Castle, young Oxford could have witnessed for himself how plays were created for the theater.

Hedingham Castle

When Edward was 12 years old, his father passed away, and then his mother remarried, which at that time meant Edward de Vere became a royal ward of Queen Elizabeth.

Oxford was sent to London to live with Queen Elizabeth's Secretary of State, William Cecil and his wife Mildred. The two raised the boy at a mansion called Cecil House.

Given a study schedule, Oxford had lessons in Latin and French for two hours each day, as well as daily sessions in dancing, religion, writing, and music.

Oxford received an honorary degree from Cambridge at age 14 and a Master of Arts degree from Oxford University at age 16. At 17, Oxford studied law at Gray's Inn. (The picture below is Hedingham today.) Back then, the law was written in Latin, so Oxford HAD to be an expert in Latin to attend law school.

Arthur Golding, the man credited for first translating Ovid's *Metamorphosis* from Latin to English, was not only Oxford's maternal uncle, but the two lived together at Cecil House while Golding was translating *Metamorphosis*.

Might hearing his uncle talk about the 15-book poem have sparked an interest in Oxford to want to read it? Cecil House contained one of the finest libraries in the world. So, there were two editions of *Metamorphosis* there, plus, Edward did not need to walk miles to school. He would step down the stairs where tutors would instruct him. Can we prove with 100% certainty that Oxford read these books? No, so, like the Folger, he "almost certainly" read them with a cup of tea in the comfort of his home.

If Mr. Monk were investigating this case, he might proclaim: "The plots for all of Shakespeare's plays were stolen from Greek and Latin books and not original." This is true.

The real author "borrowed" stories found in ancient books, and modern academics have tracked down the sources. Many were *only* written in Greek or Latin, which is why the "real" author must have had *an extensive* knowledge of Latin and Greek.

But in the preface to the First Folio, Ben Jonson famously claimed that William Shakespeare knew "small Latin and less Greek."

This raises the question: how would Stratford be able to read the sources for the plays if he knew "little" or "small" Latin and less Greek? Plus, where would he find books written in Greek?

Would they be very common?

We will return to this subject a little later on.

Is this Circumstantial Evidence?

Did you know 26-year-old Anne Hathaway was already three months pregnant at her wedding to 18-year-old William Shakespeare in November of 1582?

So, do you think William may have spent his free time wooing Anne, at her farm, because they lived in a strict religious society?

Back in those times did most women believe in having premarital sex? No. But apparently, Stratford really knew how to spread those "thy's."

Because William had not turned 21, the church required a marriage bond, which Fulk Sandells and John Richardson agreed to sign as guarantors. Both men were farmers from Shottery, the town where Anne Hathaway lived. They were trusted friends of the bride's father, but, if William Shakespeare had been spending hours at school reading books in Latin, how would he get to know these two farmers?

If William was living on Henley Street, why didn't he ask Richard Hornby and Edward Willes to be his witnesses? They were John Shakespeare's two adjoining neighbors on Henley Street. But he did not. Instead, two farmers who lived two hours from town agreed to guarantee the bond payment for an apparent stranger.

Even if they personally liked Anne and did not want to see her pregnant and unwed these men would stand to lose £40 if William were not of good character. Back then £40 was a lot of money. It was about $25,000 in today's money and enough to purchase an average house.

So, was William Shakespeare really spending his free time writing poetry and reading books? Or was he spending his free time humping, banging, and shagging his future wife? Don't answer that.

However, most Stratford scholars focus on the plays and will NOT even mention that in order for Shakespeare to write **two long poems** before 1594 he HAD to read over 40 books. And some were written in Spanish and Italian. Is this true?

A wealth of plays

Shakespeare was an extremely versatile playwright, constantly experimentting with new styles of drama and developing his range of subject matter and the depth of understanding of character throughout his career. His first plays include the light comedies *The Two Gentlemen of Verona* and *The Taming of the Shrew*, the bloody tragedy of *Titus Andronicus*, and four plays, also more or less tragic in form, based on English history -- three on the reign of Henry VI and a follow-up about Richard III.

All these were written before the founding of the Lord Chamberlain's Men in 1594. The end of that year saw a performance of this brilliantly plotted *Comedy of Errors*, in which he interweaves a tale of mistaken identity derived from Roman comedy with the romantic tale of a family parted but eventually reunited.

from *The Shakespeare Book- Big Ideas Simply Explained* by Pr. Said Farkane. With Contributions from Sir Stanley Wells & Paul Edmondson

7

Lost Years or Forgotten Poems?

When we last left him, two trusted Hathaway friends had guaranteed a marriage bond for William Shakespeare so he could marry Anne Hathaway. The wedding took place in November of 1582.

Then, on May 26, 1583, according to the Folger, Will and Anne baptized first daughter Susanna "Shaksper". Two years later, the Folger tells us that Anne and William became the proud parents of twins: Hamnet and Judith who were baptized on Feb 2, 1585.

Then in 1587, came a lawsuit involving John and William Shakespeare. Most likely, William stayed around a year for that.

Then, abracadabra! William vanishes! William of Stratford disappears from all documented records, leaving behind a wife with three young children to raise as a single parent.

What happened to him? Where did he go?

Did William work as a schoolteacher in the country? Could he have sailed to Italy and back? Or did he join the British Navy to fight against the Spanish Armada? Most scholars point out these "lost years" as the golden-ticket answer to everything. Instead of speculating on these years, let us look at his two forgotten poems to see if we can find any evidence to solve our cold case mystery. I call these two poems forgotten because they are often overlooked. They are usually omitted from the chronology of plays and as a result, people forget about them. Today we are going to view the source materials of these two long poems as well as one of the plays.

According to Sir Stanley Wells, between 1591 – 1594, William Shakespeare wrote seven plays:

1. *Henry VI Part 1,*
2. *Henry VI Part 2*
3. *Henry VI Part 3*
4. *Titus Andronicus,*
5. *Richard III,*
6. *Edward III*
7. *The Comedy of Errors.*

But Sir Stanley failed to mention the two forgotten poems.

Now, if Mr. Monk were examining the case, he would point out something obvious: "Whoever wrote the poems *Venus & Adonis* and *The Rape of Lucrece* had to be *an expert in Latin and Greek* because it would have taken hundreds of hours to write these two poems. Plus, many of the source books had yet-to-be-translated into English."

So, let us examine the foundations of the two poems.

The Rape of Lucrece has two main sources: *The Fasti* by Ovid and *The History of Rome* by Livy. *The Fasti* consists of six books and was first translated from Latin into English **in 1640** while *The History of Rome* by Livy has 35+ books and tells the story of the founding of Rome. It was first translated from Latin to English in the year **1600**.

It seems like a stretch to say *all* thirty-five of Livy's books were used to write *The Rape of Lucrece*, so let us say that the poet used 12 of the 35 books. So, 12 books + 6 = 18 Latin books for just one poem, *The Rape of Lucrece.*

The main source for *Venus and Adonis* is Book 10 of Ovid's 15 book masterpiece, *Metamorphosis* which Arthur Golding first translated from Latin into English in 1567.

But would not Shakespeare need to read all 15 books first?

We know he read Book 4 because the play *Titus Andronicus* was first performed in 1593 and it was based on Book 4 of *Metamorphoses.*

Therefore, not just "anybody" could have written the Shakespeare canon because it takes time to translate books from Latin into English and then to write poems and plays.

Still, some of you might claim the Bard could have taught himself Greek and Latin during the lost years, right?

(I knew it!)

For those of you thinking he was a "self-taught genus" Mr. Monk might have you consider the play *The Comedy of Errors*.

First performed on December 27, 1594, this play had to be written *before December 27, 1594.*

[Obviously, the play also had to be performed before the Queen's censor too, as the actors could not just show up in costume somewhere to perform something.]

The Comedy of Errors was based on *Menaechmi* by Plautus which was not translated from Latin to English until *after* 1594.

So, add another Latin book to the slush pile to translate and read. Plus, *The Comedy of Errors* boasts legal jargon, puns, and jokes about the law, so, would not the author need to be "self-taught" in the law?

When we add up all the volumes from Latin to English needed to write just two long poems and one play, we find that a total of 20 books all written in Latin would need to be translated into English before he could start writing *Lucrece*. But remember, this poem came out in 1594, and it was published and printed less than one year after the 1593 publication of *Venus & Adonis*.

Remember, 15 books of the *Metamorphoses* had to be read first to write *Venus & Adonis* which was printed in 1593. But that is not all folks! What about *The Comedy of Errors*? It was first performed on December 27 of 1594.

Plus, Stratford experts (not me) claim that during this time, Stratford's company The Chamberlain's Men staged plays almost every single day in 1594 (from the summer to the end of the year.)

Experts say that William Shakespeare's name got added to the Queen's payment list which proves he **also acted** in the plays.

When you realize the amount of books he would need to translate and devour, would the real author have time to do all this without an amazing knowledge of Latin?

Did Stratford have amazing language skills? No.

Edward de Vere was 14 years older than William Shakespeare. He started learning Latin at age four and continued for two hours a day till he was 21 years old. Shakespeare might have started at age 12 but quickly tapped out. Even if he had a photographic memory, learning a foreign language involves practicing, drilling, and rehearsing with a tutor or mentor. Plus, where could William go to find and read several obscure books in Spanish?

Yes, Spanish. Some of the source books are in Spanish.

It is kind of like my wife and I speaking Spanish. I took 3 years of Español in high school, and I have picked up even more vocabulary after being married. So, I think I can speak the language decently enough.

One time I even beat my wife at an online Spanish test too.

Woo hoo!

My wife never took Spanish in high school; however, Spanish is her first language. She was born and raised in Guatemala so who do you think knows Spanish better, me or her? She does, right? (My friends tell me what a great wife I must have for throwing that online test just to make me look good!)

We work together selling houses and one time I got a call from a Spanish-speaking gentleman. I told my wife, "Let me handle the part where we establish rapport." She agreed.

Establishing rapport means you pick out an object in a house like golf clubs and ask, "Do you like to play golf? I do too." You share something in common to help break the ice.

When we entered the house, the owners' two small poodles approached me.

They had recently been groomed, so I bent down to pet them and said, "Sus perros huelen rico" – "Your dogs smell good."

But I have a tough time rolling my "r's," so it came out, "Sus **pedos** huelen rico."

Instantly I noticed a sparkle in the man's eyes. His wife smiled and my wife rolled her eyes, so I knew I had misspoken. But we just went on from there.

We left the place and on the ride home, my wife asked, "Do you know what you told them when they first greeted us?" "Yes," I said, "Your dogs smell good." She said, "Nope, you said 'pedos,' we all heard you."

I said, "Okay, maybe I did say pedos."

She grinned at me and said, "Don't get mad at me, but you told them, 'Your farts smell delicious'".

This is not embarrassing at all, is it?

I mention this story because am I the only person who has ever made a mistake learning another language? No.

But William Shakespeare? He can take a few weeks of Latin, and translate 40 books into English and then pen two long poems and several plays perfectly. Including one about the law: a subject he never even studied. Not in school. Not at home. No where.

I do not buy it. Does not writing involve making mistakes and fixing them? Ironing out the blunders and missteps? But that is not all folks!

Remember, we have not even talked about the sweet reading materials for the other SIX plays he wrote between 1591 – 1594!

We just did one play and two long poems.

You can Google the sources for Shakespeare's poems and plays to see for yourself! Or check out my cool chronology chart which includes not only the name of the work and when the work was written, but also the source materials for it.

Date Written	Name of Work	Source Material(s)
	Two Noble Kinsmen	Chaucer/ Boccaccio
1589-1591	The Two Gentlemen of Verona	Diana Enamorada (in Spanish) Decameron by Boccaccio
1590-1591	The Taming of the Shrew	Suppositi (in Italian) by Ariosto
1591	Henry VI Part 2	Holinshed's Chronicles (15 books)
1591	Henry VI Part 3	Holinshed's Chronicles
1591-1592	Henry VI Part 1	Holinshed's Chronicles
1591-1592	Titus Andronicus	Euripides' Hecuba, Seneca's Thyestes and Troades, Ovid's Metamorphoses
1592	**Venus & Adonis** 15 books	Metamorphoses by Ovid (Book 10 of 15 books)
1592-1593	Richard III	Holinshed's Chronicles
1592-1593	Edward III	Holinshed's Chronicles
1593	**The Rape of Lucrece** 12 books?	The History of Rome in Latin. The Fasti by Ovid
1594	The Comedy of Errors	The Menaechmi by Plautus
1594-1595	Love's Labour's Lost	Works by Sir Philip Sidney and John Lyly
1594-1595	Love's Labour Won	This play might have been renamed but it's lost
1595	Richard II	Holinshed's Chronicles
1595	Romeo & Juliet	Matteo Bandello and Arthur Brooke

Did William Shakespeare of Stratford *have the time* to self-teach himself Latin and the law as well as do all this translating, reading, writing, and rewriting?

No, and because he lacked the books, an extensive Latin education, and the time to rewrite, the evidence points to him NOT being the author.

Still, to most die-hard fans, this is not proof of anything.

Many will insist that geniuses have incomprehensible powers, or they will tell me Stratford's name on the First Folio shows he has a "prima facie" case of authorship and that is good enough for them. What is a prima facie case?

8

Prima Facie & Three Questions

What does a prima facie case for authorship mean? Prima facie means "at first glance" or "accepted as correct until proven otherwise" but it does NOT mean absolute certainty.

A woman sees her boyfriend entertaining another woman at a restaurant. This is a good example of a prima facie case or the plot of a Hallmark movie. She saw him with her own eyes. End of story. But what if the other woman was his sister or his business client?

Many experts claim that Shakespeare's authorship is a foregone conclusion because they see his name listed as the author and that is all the direct evidence they need. Some will claim stylometry and handwriting analysis bolster their claim. But like the wife who sees her husband with another woman, it all depends on the identity of the other woman, doesn't it?

Not every book can be judged by its cover.

What is Stylometry?

Stylometry is a modern approach to identify an author which uses statistics that are based on the number of times an author employs three letter words (like "the" or "and") and/or two letter words like "an" or "by." Allegedly, every author has a unique fingerprint depending on the number of times two, three- and four-letter words are used. These days, many readers believe anything analyzed by a computer to be more precise. A computer algorithm seems more impersonal, professional, and effective.

However, the adage about "garbage going in equals garbage going out" still rings true. In Stylometry, a large sample size of data is needed to make an accurate comparison, otherwise it is agreed, the computer algorithm for identifying an author does not work. The computer will be comparing apples with oranges.

Shakespeare's plays, poems and sonnets combine to over one million words. This is a huge data set, but not even one handwritten letter by the Bard survives to this day. We cannot even compare Shakespeare's own handwritten words to the Shakespeare canon!

What happens when experts compare Edward de Vere's writing to the Shakespeare canon? Two words: Insufficient data. We have a data set of sixteen de Vere poems to use. Experts are not even sure if his sixteen rhymes are poems or songs because Edward de Vere's poems are found in a book filled with songs.

So, is it truly accurate to compare de Vere's poetic works to Shakespeare's? No.

What about Handwriting Analysis?

No letters, diaries or other documents exist that are known to have been written 100% by William Shakespeare. Only six childish signatures taken from legal documents exist. So, again, we have insufficient data.

Still, there are those who will *never* doubt that Stratford was the real author. They will die on this hill and claim that a play called "Sir Thomas Moore" was written by the Bard and the handwriting of "Hand D" can be compared favorably to his six shaky signatures.

However, modern forensic handwriting experts do NOT agree. Insufficient data strikes again.

Therefore, in this chapter, I will ask three questions for those who believe in William of Stratford's authorship in hopes that you will look beyond the author's name on the cover of a book.

Question#1: How did Shakespeare know Rosenkrantz and Guildenstern? Nowadays most people know that Detective Adrian Monk is a fictional TV character but what about Rosenkrantz and Guildenstern? These characters can be found in the play *Hamlet*, as well as in a play by Tom Stoppard, *Rosenkrantz and Guildenstern are Dead.*

Were you aware that Rosencrantz and Guildenstern were two living, breathing people?

The diplomat, Peregrine Bertie, English ambassador to Denmark, recorded in 1582 that he met with Rosenkrantz and two men with the surname of Guildenstern, along with King Frederick II at a royal dinner party in Denmark.

They were NOT characters from a play; they were the Danish king's actual courtiers. I mention this because some people have long wondered how the author of *Hamlet* could have known about the peculiar details of Danish royal culture.

The King of Denmark's drinking ritual involved firing cannon blasts with every downed shot of liquor. Shakespeare writes:

No jocund health that Denmark drinks today, But the great cannon to the clouds shall tell, And the King's rouse the heavens shall bruit again, Re-speaking earthly thunder. Come away. (Ham I.ii.123-128)

Peregrine Bertie knew about this true-to-life drinking game of the Danish king, because of his two visits to Denmark. He had stayed in Denmark for over six months on each trip. What is Peregrine Bertie's relationship to William of Stratford-upon-Avon? Zilch. Zero. Nada. Bertie had NO connection to the Stratford man. Plus, at that time, the cannon shots were NOT documented in any books. But Peregrine Bertie *was married* to Edward de Vere's sister.

Could Peregrine Bertie have regaled Oxford with stories about his visits to Denmark and his meetings with King Frederick II? Did Bertie give him the quirky names Rosenkrantz and Guildenstern?

Question#2: Why So Much Fainting in the Canon? Ever notice all the fainting that happens in the Shakespeare canon? Experts claim the "real" author wrote thirty-seven plays but guess what happens in nine of them? People faint, swoon, or "sound."

This means that there is almost a 25% chance that when you watch a Shakespeare play, an actor will faint on stage.

When asked about this, some scholars will say, "that's just how plays were written back then." But does that make sense?

If other playwrights were NOT doing it, then it was NOT how plays were written.

Also, swooning happens not only in the "real" author's plays, but in **his poetry** too. Not his Sonnets. Here is what I am referring to:

In *Anthony & Cleopatra,* Cleopatra faints.
In *As You Like It*, Rosalind faints.
In *Much Ado About Nothing*, Hero swoons
In *Henry VI,* Clifford faints.
In *Henry VI*, The King swoons.
In *King Lear*, King Lear faints.
In *Othello*, Roderigo faints.
In *Pericles*, Thaisa faints.
In *The Winter's Tale* Hermione faints.
The poem "*The Passionate Pilgrim*" has a line, "To sin and never for to faint."
In *The Rape of Lucrece*, there are two fainters: "Here manly Hector faints." And Tarquin, "As if with grief or travel he had fainted, to me came Tarquin armed to beguiled."
In the poem, *Venus & Adonis*, Venus says, "Didst thou not mark my face? was it not white? Sawst thou not sign of fear

> lurk in mine eye? Grew I not faint? and fell I not downright?
> (*V&A* 644)

Please note I did not include ALL the fainting. Dr. Kenneth W. Heaton, a British physician, once read every line of Shakespeare's works and in 2006 proclaimed: "Shakespeare recorded fainting under strong emotion on **18 occasions**, with near fainting on 13 occasions."

(See "A List of Links and Sources" at the back of this book.)

Again, why so much fainting? Me? I am not a physician, but could it be that the "real" author experienced it in his own life? If so, was it because he had fainted as a child?

Modern psychiatric studies indicate that a high percentage of the time, seizure disorders can be linked to **epilepsy** and then to adult episodes of **bipolar disorder**. In other words, a current theory is that pediatric epilepsy does not get "cured," it simply morphs into schizophrenia or bipolar disorder.

Recent findings appearing in *Molecular Psychiatry* indicate a gene called ANK3 was found in some people having epilepsy. This gene mutated. Soon afterward, ANK3 was later linked to bipolar disorder.

So, if the "real" author had endured episodes of epilepsy as a child, did he also experience bipolar disorder as an adult? Or vice versa?

If he experienced bipolar disorder as an adult, did he endure epilepsy as a child? How would we know today, 400+ years later?

One of the Elizabethan tonics for epilepsy was "mumia" or "mummy" which is mentioned in three of Shakespeare's plays. We see it in *Othello* where the audience discovers that Othello's mother's handkerchief had been dyed in mummy. What was Mummy?

A Mummy

Made from the bodies of dead humans, apothecaries would grind up the embalmed cloth and sell it for big money. Mummies were an important ingredient in medicines.

Mummy exuded a foul, pungent odor. It smelled like hot asphalt or tar so a handkerchief was often dipped into a bowl of the human remains and placed under the nose of the person like smelling salts for an epileptic person. Or people would eat it.

Could Stratford have learned about mummy during his "lost" years? It is possible, but remember, it cost a pretty penny to buy mummy because it got shipped all the way from Egypt!

But we know Edward de Vere lived with Queen Elizabeth's right-hand-man, so if Edward had been treated for seizures at an early age, what would the royal physician have treated him with? Mummy.

It is important to point out that not one person in history has ever accused Edward de Vere of mental illness. Who died and made me Freud? Nobody. I am just pointing out what seems obvious. Also, does not an epilepsy/bipolar disorder combo seem like a fingerprint?

Researchers claim the number of people with this rare combination is less than 0.05% of the world's population. We will talk more about these things later in this book, so for now, let us move onto the next question.

Question #3: How would Stratford know about 'Scented' Gloves? According to English historian John Stow, upon his return from Italy in 1576, Edward de Vere introduced several Italian luxury items to the English court which quickly became fashionable. One was embroidered or trimmed 'scented' gloves.

Queen Elizabeth received one pair of these gloves scented with perfume that for many years was known as the "Earl of Oxford's perfume." Why do I mention this?

In *The Winter's Tale*, we hear of perfumed gloves when Mopsa says,

"I have done. Come, you promised me a tawdry-lace and a pair of sweet (scented) Gloves." (WT. IV. 4. 248)

Why scented gloves?

Stratford-lovers may laugh and say, "Yeah, well William's father was a glover. So, of course he would know all about "sweet" scented gloves!" But would he? Remember, John Shakespeare had called himself a glover in 1556 eight years before William was born. Then, according to the Folger, John called himself a yeoman, and others called him a "whittawer" (leather worker) "usurer" (moneylender) or a "wool dealer."

If Shakespeare was the real author, and we know he was from Warwickshire and had never visited Italy where scented gloves were the fashion, why wouldn't it be a pair of "doeskin" gloves?

Do These Thoughts Resonate?

Peregrine Bertie who had personally met Rosenkrantz and Guildenstern had no ties to Stratford.

Fainting is found in poems of the real author as well as his plays.

Recent findings appearing in *Molecular Psychiatry* indicate a gene called ANK3 mutated in some people with epilepsy. Soon afterward, ANK3 was also connected to bipolar disorder.

Scented gloves were a present to Queen Elizabeth from Oxford and not Stratford.

Like an old mummy, this chapter is officially a wrap. Moving along, let us talk more about mental health.

9

Mr. Monk's Mental Illness

If you have ever watched the TV show Monk, you may recall that Monk's obsession with symmetry, various phobias, fear of germs, and contamination seem to help him. Even though Adrian Monk cannot drive a car it does not stop him from solving crimes. He has a devoted and capable assistant in Natalie Teeger and in the early episodes, Sharona who would drive for him.

My point is, just like Monk, even if the "real" author of the Shakespeare canon endured mental illness it would *not* stop him from writing plays, poems, or doing anything he loved.

How is this related to our cold case mystery?

Back in early March of 2020, the state of California shut down like Blockbuster Video for the COVID pandemic. During this time, I stayed home and watched TV and it was then I started noticing all the daytime TV commercials for the drug Latuda. It seemed like every other advert featured the same young woman hawking the medication.

Curious, I pulled out my iPhone and clicked on the Latuda website. What is Latuda? How much does it cost? Answer: Latuda costs about $1,500 for a one month's supply. It is used to treat people with bipolar disorder. What is bipolar disorder?

Bipolar Disorder or "BD" is a mood disorder associated with feelings of extreme highs followed by weeks of depression or melancholy. BD used to be called manic depression.

The same day, while doom-scrolling on Twitter I watched a video of actor Patrick Stewart reading a Shakespeare sonnet. During the pandemic he would read "a sonnet a day" and listening to him made me pause.

I noticed how the "real" author talked about feeling shameful, in deep despair, and wanting to die. I could not help but think to myself. Wow. *This dude sounds like he could use some Latuda!* Then I realized something. What if the real author had endured some form of bipolar disorder? Obviously, I am not a doctor but wouldn't something like a rare mood disorder shown in the Bard's writing be like a fingerprint to help solve our cold case? Here is the Shakespeare sonnet I heard:

> Tired with all these, for restful death I cry,
> As, to behold desert a beggar born,
> And needy nothing trimmed in jollity,
> And purest faith unhappily forsworn,
> And gilded honour shamefully misplaced,
> And maiden virtue rudely strumpeted,
> And right perfection wrongfully disgraced,
> And strength by limping sway disabled,
> And art made tongue-tied by authority,
> And folly, doctor-like, controlling skill,
> And simple truth miscalled simplicity,
> And captive good attending captain ill.
> Tired with all these, from these would I be gone,
> Save that, to die, I leave my love alone.

Some people will argue that poets who wrote sonnets during the Elizabethan era wanted to sound "dramatic," so this was just "the style" back then.

But why do we automatically assume this to be true? What if the author had only jotted down his true, private feelings? They were only for himself or his friends?

And, what if Edward de Vere had epilepsy as a child but Queen Elizabeth had ordered him never to talk about his seizures or she would have him committed to a mental institution?

If so, might writing a play about depression be like tweeting about his miserable day publicly on Twitter?

Might covertly writing a sonnet about his pessimistic feelings make him feel slightly better?

The sad reality is that back then, most mentally ill patients were feared by people, so they were locked up.

The most popular 'treatment' drew on a medieval understanding of madness as **demonic possession**. This meant that an evil spirit possessing a victim had to be forced out, usually with violence.

In the play, *As You Like It,* Rosalind remarks, "lovers, like madmen, deserve 'a dark house and a whip' (AYLI, 3.2.401). In *The Comedy of Errors*, Dr. Pinch misdiagnoses Antipholus and Dromio of Ephesus as possessed: 'I know it by their pale and deadly looks [;] / They must be bound and laid in some dark room' (COE 4.4.88–89).

Beaten with a stick and then bound and laid in some "dark" room was the textbook treatment for bipolar disorder patients.

10

Four Manic Symptoms

Bipolar disorder used to be called "manic depression" and it involves two types of episodes: manic and depressive. In this chapter, we will focus only on the manic symptoms which can last for a few days or a week. This list of manic symptoms comes from the US National Survey on Drug Use and Health or NSDUH. The four manic symptoms include:

Symptom #1: An increase in energy.

Extra energy can manifest in several unusual ways, and can include feeling more awake, hyper, or having out-of-control feelings, not unlike those by an adrenaline rush.

Symptom #2: A decreased need for sleep.

In manic episodes, many people feel as though they need little sleep. An optimal level may mean only a few hours of sleep or can result in a complete avoidance of sleep.

Symptom #3: Impulsive behavior.

During manic episodes impulsive behavior can lead to gambling, reckless spending, reckless sexual behaviors, criminal activity, and dangerous physical activity. Things like skipping school or sluffing off work may happen.

Symptom #4: Racing thoughts, heart rate, and speech patterns.

Many people with bipolar disorder may feel as though their thoughts are moving at one million miles an hour. Their heart rate might be similarly elevated, and the combination of elevated heart rate and racing thoughts can lead to fainting spells, unusual speech patterns, such as speaking extremely quickly or jumping from topic to topic, and no longer making sense.

Question: Did William Shakespeare of Stratford-upon-Avon exhibit any of these symptoms? **No.** He did not.

[At least not of which we are aware.]

But Edward de Vere was **renowned** for doing things that today we might call "manic" episodes. He was legendary. Take for example reckless spending. How might a legend spend money?

Well, at age 21, Oxford inherited an estate worth about seventy million dollars, in today's money. Ten years later, Oxford was almost completely broke. Is that a good example of reckless spending? Author Alan H. Nelson wrote an autobiography of de Vere called *Monstrous Adversary.*

The word, **"monstrous"** means "having the frightening or ugly appearance of a monster; inhumanly evil or dangerous." Does this describe how most people viewed someone with bipolar disorder?

Nelson claims in 1583, Oxford's father-in-law described Oxford as being "almost bankrupt" and "only having four servants." (Oxford inherited his money in 1571 when he turned 21.) So, he blew through $70 million dollars in ten years! Now, that is epic!

Nelson's unflattering portrait of Oxford shows him to be "self-indulgent," "erratic" and "belligerent with a tendency towards violence."

At tilt tournaments, Oxford excelled at "jousting," an incredibly dangerous sport where two horsemen ride at full speed with a long lance (or spear) and try to "unhorse" the other rider. Are dangerous physical activities symptoms of bipolar disorder? Yes.

In 1578, the writer Gabriel Harvey described the suicidal style of the jousting champion Edward de Vere as: "thy countenance shakes spears." (Other men holding spears are afraid of you!)

Do you recall that manic bipolar symptoms include reckless sexual behavior? Oxford allegedly not only had sex with female prostitutes, but according to his cousin, males too, including a young Italian boy Oxford brought back to England while he was married. Oxford never denied it.

Then when Oxford was older, he became deeply religious: there were two sides to him like Dr. Jekyll and Mr. Hyde.

But these are all "manic" symptoms. If Oxford truly were bipolar, would he not also exhibit "depressive" symptoms?

11

Six Depressive Symptoms

A "depressive" episode means the exact opposite of a manic episode and is often characterized by a prolonged period of sadness, despair, or apathy. It can last between 1 to 3 weeks.

And in Bipolar II Disorder, depressive episodes can last even longer! Per the National Survey on Drug Use and Health, the six symptoms of a depressive episode include:

#1: Lack of energy. People find it difficult to do activities that were previously enjoyed. This lack of energy can make it difficult to get out of bed in the morning and can make even getting dressed and eating difficult to do.

#2: Insomnia Depression can result in an increased need for sleep, as well as a decreased ability to sleep.

#3: Feelings of Worthlessness and Guilt. People during a depressive episode might experience overwhelming feelings of guilt or worthlessness.

#4: Extreme Sadness or Despair. Bipolar disorder's depressive episodes can result in feelings of despair, and the sadness may seem overwhelming.

#5: Agitated Depression, Feelings of Guilt and/or Paranoia: Agitated depression is not a medical term, but some people use it to describe this combination of anxiety and depression. It is a mixture that often involves anger and restlessness, then afterwards feelings of regret, guilt, and paranoia.

#6: Thoughts of Suicide. Thoughts of self-harming are depressive symptoms with irritability, distractibility, and psychomotor agitation present in 90% of attempters.

Did William Shakespeare of Stratford-upon-Avon exhibit any "depressive" episodes that historians have noted? **None.**

In the title page of a poem found in the First Folio, Ben Johnson described William Shakespeare as "gentle", and yes it is true, a lot of bipolar people can be "gentle".

Stratford did, however, gift Anne Hathaway a "second-best" bed in his will, but even that is argued by most researchers as not a snub. According to the Shakespeare Birthplace Trust: In Elizabethan days, a bed was "an expensive and luxurious item, regarded as a valuable heirloom to be passed down the generations rather than given to a surviving spouse."

Therefore, William Shakespeare was NOT being vindictive or exhibiting a depressive episode by passing down their tired, old, marriage bed.

However, books were worth good money back in those days, so it does seem odd that he would gift his wife with an old bed but not any used books that she might be able to resell for a tidy profit.

Circumstantial Evidence for Oxford?

In his youth, according to his biographer, Oxford was mysteriously ill for several weeks at a time. Alan H. Nelson speculates that Oxford may have been in quarantine, but could he not have been depressed and feeling no or low energy?

Nelson writes that Oxford "was chronically sickly, hypochondriacal or both." Chronically sick means persistently, habitually, frequently and continuously, doesn't it?

We know Oxford spent money excessively like an inveterate gambler or someone who is always ready to roll the dice because Nelson writes:

A conspicuous consumer, over nine months Oxford purchased 32 pairs of Spanish shoes, nine pantoffles (a kind of slipper), three Moyles (a kind of shoe), six hats, five capes, and seven pairs of garters. ... Oxford lay sick at Windsor for part of the first term, and at Charing Cross, evidently again for illness, for some of the second. From his outlays on drugs and care, at £66-16-0, nearly one-fifth of his total expenses, and from his subsequent patronage of apothecaries, we may infer that Oxford was chronically sick, hypochondrial or both.

Hmm. From this passage we learn that Oxford visited apothecaries often and he purchased a total of forty-four pairs of shoes in nine months. Did he really need all these shoes? No.

Edward de Vere engaged in what my wife likes to call **retail-therapy**, aka stress-shopping!

Buying shoes made him feel better! Or was it the shopping? Also, the table of contents taken from Nelson's biography of adult Edward de Vere does show a weepy, Eeyorish side.

From letters written by Edward de Vere, we find chapter headings labeled:

I have not an Able Body

Deep Abyss

Bottom of Despair.

So, fellow detectives, did Edward de Vere experience bipolar disorder? It seems possible because his real-life actions certainly displayed the classic symptoms. They are also a match to the feelings of despair of the author of the Shakespeare canon. I believe the symptoms of epilepsy and bipolar disorder prove that he and the "real" author were one and the same person.

However, many Oxfordians and Stratfordians are reluctant to change and unwilling to admit the possibility that William Shakespeare aka Edward de Vere experienced bipolar disorder.

They will say, "How is it possible to accurately diagnose any person who died four hundred years ago with bipolar disorder?" But is this true?

Unlike a COVID test, where a swab of cotton can react instantaneously with COVID antibodies, there is **no similar medical test** for bipolar disorder.

Instead, anyone may take an online test which asks a series of questions.to find out if their results are consistent with bipolar disorder. Here is an example of the questions:

- Ever felt that nothing could make you happy or joyful?
- Ever experience feelings of anguish or desperation?
- Were you aggressive or violent towards others?

We just saw how Allan H. Nelson used words from de Vere's own letters to write chapter headings:

I have not an Able Body

Deep Abyss

Bottom of Despair

Nelson also wrote Oxford was "belligerent with a tendency towards violence."

Therefore, if someone like me answered them truthfully as Edward de Vere, am I guilty of misdiagnosing Edward de Vere? Or is the website algorithm correct in telling us Edward de Vere's results **indicate** a **high risk** of bipolar disorder?

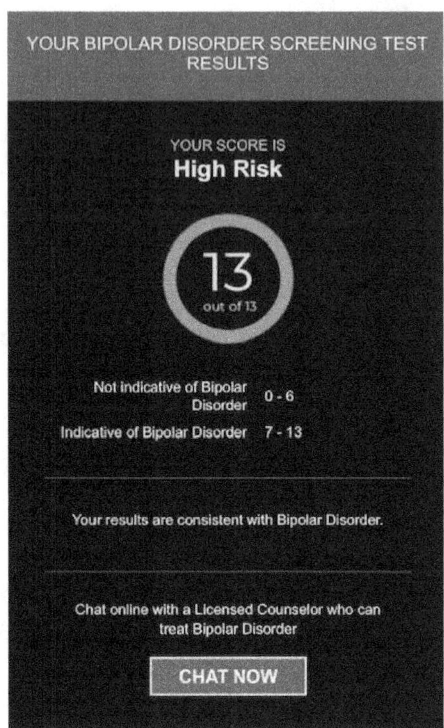

According to this test, Oxford's results DO show a high risk of bipolar disorder. So, his next step today would be to chat with a licensed therapist or healthcare professional.

But again, there is no quantitative test TODAY to diagnose someone with bipolar disorder. Sad but true. In the year 2021, there are websites raising money to fund "a quest for the test".

Parents of children who have died taking their own lives due to bipolar disorder are trying to make the public aware that there needs to be a verifiable medical test for this disorder.

Therefore, I reached out to several psychiatrists to ask their professional opinions. One doctor who wishes to remain anonymous emailed: "*You may be the first person to suggest that the Earl of Oxford had bipolar disorder. While it is exceedingly difficult to make a diagnosis across centuries and without a full medical examination, your hypothesis might be strengthened by including the possibility of Bipolar II Disorder. Here is a link to the diagnostic criteria in the current DSM-5 manual."* And he provided the link. Here it is for you: https://www.psychiatry.org/psychiatrists/practice/dsm

Do These Thoughts Resonate?

- Edward de Vere had an extensive education that included two hours a day of learning Latin and French.
- He was known for writing the best poetry at Queen Elizabeth's court.
- Oxford did not have to worry about money, so he had time to devote to reading and writing.
- Oxford had access to information at his fingertips that Stratford did not have.
- Oxford exhibited highs and lows like someone with bipolar mood disorder, and frequent fainting and talk about "melancholy" mentioned in the Shakespeare canon indicates that its author was familiar with it.

12

Oxford's Poetry

Did you know that most of Oxford's poems were written before his 16th birthday? Some of them were compiled for a book while he was still a teenager by the choirmaster of the Royal Chapel, Richard Edwards. After Edward turned twenty-six, he stopped writing poetry. Why?

Most standard-issue Oxford fans will claim he stopped because Oxford started writing under a different name: a pseudonym named William Shakespeare.

But if Edward de Vere was the "real" author and he passed away in 1604, and William Shakespeare did not die until 1616, why didn't Oxford's wife object to Stratford's identity theft? Why did she keep silent if she knew Shakespeare was not the real author? We will discuss this issue later.

My question to you is this: are *bipolar symptoms* in the poems of young Oxford like those expressed by the "real" author? Do they illuminate the speaker's fragile mental health? Do his words talk about symptoms such as deep distress, sadness, and worthlessness? Do they talk about someone who never gets to present his true self to others?

Here are some of Oxford's poems, so you can see for yourself. They all come from a book titled *The Paradise of Dainty Devises* (1576). What is interesting is that the lyrics for a song called *Griping Grief* found in the play *Romeo & Juliet* comes from the same book which contains sixteen poems/songs written by Edward de Vere. Like singer Kurt Cobain from the band Nirvana who was also bipolar, Edward de Vere found solace in music. He played the lute. The first poem by Edward de Vere is called *Loss of Good Name*

.

> Framed in the front of forlorn hope,
> past all recovery,
> I stayless stand to abide the shock
> of shame and infamy.
> My life through lingering long
> is lodged, in lair of loathsome ways,
> My death delayed to keep from life,
> the harm of hapless days.
> My spirits, my heart, my wit,
> and force, in deep distress are drowned,
> The only loss of my good name
> is of these griefs the ground. —Earl of Oxford

Notice Oxford's use of alliteration? Alliteration is defined as "the occurrence of the same letter or sound at the beginning of adjacent or closely connected words. An example of alliteration might be "*Griping Griefs*." Also, Oxford does sound a lot like a doleful person who is feeling melancholy, doesn't he?

In this next excerpt, notice how young Oxford complains of insomnia or not getting enough sleep. Is not sleeping a symptom of bipolar disorder? And there was no such thing as Ambien.

> My meaning is to work
> what wonders love hath wrought,

Wherewith I muse why men of wit
have love so dearly bought.
For love is worse than hate,
and ere more harm hath done
Record I take of those that read of Paris,
Priam's son. It seemed the God of sleep
had mazed so much his wits,
When he refused wit for love,
which cometh but by fits,
But why accuse I him,
whom earth hath covered long?
There be of his posterity alive,
I do him wrong.

Here we see young Oxford alluding to ancient Greece. This is something Shakespeare liked to do. For example, there are 53 classical allusions in *Titus Andronicus*; 39 in *Antony and Cleopatra*; 38 in *Love's Labour Lost;* 37 in *A Midsummer Night's Dream;* 31 in *Cymberline;* 26 in *Coriolanus;* 25 in *Romeo and Juliet;* 25 in *All's Well that Ends Well*; 25 in *Pericles*; 19 in *Hamlet*; 11 in *Othello;* 8 in *Macbeth* and 8 in *King Lear*. Moving along...

We all know that the word "contented" means "happy and at ease." Besides buying shoes, what do you think will make Oxford happy? This next poem tells us. It is titled: *A Contented Mind.*

My mind to me a kingdom is
Such perfect joy there I find,
That it excels all other bliss
The world affords or grows by kind.
Though much I want which most men have,
Yet still my mind forbids to crave

No princely pomp,
No wealthy store,
No force to win the victory.
No wily wit to salve a sore,
No shape to feed each gazing eye
To none of these I yield as thrall, for why?
My mind doth serve for all.

Here we see a contented mind makes Oxford happy. What is the opposite of a contented mind? An unhappy, despondent, or depressed mind, wouldn't you agree?

Stratfordian author, Steven May discovered sixteen "youthful" poems he attributed to Oxford, and in at least five of these poems Oxford complains how *despairing* and tearful he feels about losing out in love. But what about a happy love poem?

In bipolar disorder, feelings of happiness are often mingled with sadness and are called "mixed" states. Does Oxford do this? This next poem is titled: *Love Compared to a Tennis Play.*

Whereas the heart at tennis plays,
and men to gaming fall,
Love is the court,
hope is the house,
and favour serves the ball.
The ball itself is true desert.
the line, which measure shows,
Is reason, whereon judgment looks
how players win or lose.
The jetty is deceitful guile,
the stopper, jealousy,
Which hath Sir Argus' hundred eyes

wherewith to watch and pry.
The fault, wherewith fifteen is lost,
is want of wit and sense,
And he that brings the racket in
is double diligence.
And lo, the racket is freewill,
which makes the ball rebound.
And noble beauty is the chase,
of every game the ground.
But rashness strikes the ball awry,
and where is oversight?
"A bandy ho," the people cry,
and so, the ball takes flight.
Now in the end,
good liking proves content
the game and gain.
Thus, in a tennis knit I love,
a pleasure mixed with pain.

Does a "pleasure mixed with pain" qualify as a mixed state? Last one. Here I want you to compare Oxford's lovesick, unrequited poem below to a sonnet written by the "real" author. First comes Oxford. Notice the first line of his poem.

I am not as I seem to be.
Nor when I smile, I am not glad.
A thrall although you count me free
I most in mirth, most pensive sad
I smile to shade my bitter spite.
As Hannibal that saw in sight.
His country soil.

In Carthage town.
By Roman force.
Defaced. Down.
I, Hannibal that smiles for grief,
And let you Caesar's tears suffice.
The one that laughs at his mischief,
The other all for joy that cries.
I smile to see me scorned so,
You weep for joy, to see me woe:
And I a heart by love slain dead
Presents in place of Pompey's head.

Oxford's first line, "I am not as I seem to be" resembles Iago's line in *Othello*, "I am not what I am." In that play, Iago means, "He is not truly and in essence what he pretends to be."

Also, it is interesting to find Hannibal in this poem; Hannibal experienced epilepsy. Compare this to the nostalgic, confident "older" William Shakespeare to hear his feelings about his unrequited love.

No longer mourn for me when I am dead.
Then you shall hear the surly sullen bell
Give warning to the world that I am fled
From this vile world with vilest worms to dwell.
Nay, if you read this line, remember not
The hand that writ it; for I love you so,
That I in your sweet thoughts would be forgot,
If thinking on me then should make you woe.
Oh, if (I say) you look upon this verse,
When I (perhaps) compounded am with clay,
Do not so much as my poor name rehearse,
But let your love even with my life decay,

> Lest the wise world should look into your moan,
> And mock you with me after I am gone.

Is it just a coincidence that both young Oxford and the "older" Shakespeare in Sonnet 71 vehemently complain about a woman who does not love him back?

The one that laughs at his mischief,
The other all for joy that cries.
I smile to see me scorned so,
You weep for joy, to see me woe:

Nay, if you read this line, remember not
The hand that writ it; for I love you so,
That I in your sweet thoughts would be forgot,
If thinking on me then should make you woe

Do not young Oxford's complaints sound like a match to William Shakespeare's feelings of unrequited love? They are both like a dark chocolate in that respect. The difference concerns more with the speaker's self-esteem.

Young Oxford lacks the poise and assuredness of the more mature, older Shakespeare. Why? Does writing under an assumed identity allow Oxford's self-confidence to bloom? Are there other instances of bipolar disorder symptoms that we can view that might offer evidence of this? Well, we do know that the "real" author, according to James Shapiro, wrote four plays in less than one year: *Henry V, Julius Caesar, As You Like It* and *Hamlet.* Plus, that year, he also helped to rebuild the Globe Theater in less than six months.

Could this be an example of manic energy?

But, if Oxford was "mad" or schizophrenic, might he not be good at keeping it a secret? What about keeping his true authorship a secret? Would that not pose a more massive problem?

Anne Cecil de Vere, the Countess of Oxford

13

Why Should We Care?

Ben Jonson once wrote, Shakespeare's work was "not of an age but for all time." His characters continue to resonate today in countless reinterpretations, as do his themes of honor, love, bravery, and madness. But what if students learned William Shakespeare did not write a single word of it?

It is a little embarrassing, isn't it?

But if students also discovered that the real writer behind the works of William Shakespeare was abusive to his wife, it also changes things. The lesson to be learned then might be one that goes: *"Being physically or mentally abusive is* ***not*** *normal. If this has happened to you in your life, then it is normal to seek help from a trained healthcare professional."*

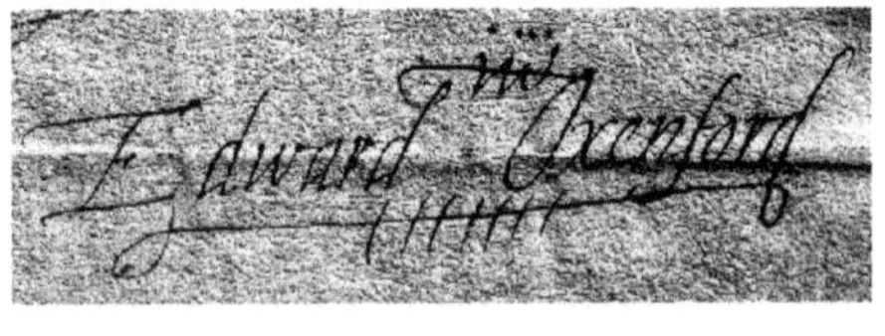

Edward de Vere signed his name "Edward Oxenford" with a little crown, and he may have grandly believed he would become the next King Edward. Grandiosity is a symptom experienced by people with bipolar disorder. Some of his actions were like those of King Edward III, who was married to Queen Phillipa of Hainault. She is regarded as the first Black queen of England. Were you aware that England once had a dark-skinned queen? She was not the monarch or ruler – her husband was, and that is why Mary Tutor, "bloody" Mary, is considered the "first" queen. Another teachable moment?

Phillipa of Hainault

Likewise, Edward de Vere fell in love with a woman named Anne Vavasour who had a "dark" (not fair) complexion, and in the Shakespeare sonnets, the author raves about a "dark" woman. Is this something that students today might relate to?

Question: when was this line written? "*Why should this rose be better esteemed than that rose, unless in pleasantness of smell it far surpasses the other rose?*" Although most people think of *Romeo & Juliet* from 1595, Edward de Vere wrote this line twenty years earlier in 1573.

Does knowing about the background of an author make the plays and poems richer and more relevant to our current times?

Unfortunately, some educators love the Bard's rags to riches story so much, that they will ignore anyone who questions his authorship. Why?

Stratfordians love the message of inclusion. They want lower-class students to believe that they too should be able to write like William Shakespeare. Yes, snobbish, high-class royals can write nicely, but so can others.

People have often used words like "should" to exclude other races, sexes, and classes. They use "should" to keep marginalized people invisible. So, I understand why educators want to hold onto this myth. It gives hope to people of color that they too can write like Shakespeare.

For centuries, "shoulds" have made an imprint on culture. What a president "should" look like. What a female "should" or "should not" be able to do. What people of color, sexual orientation, and/or disabilities should be able to accomplish? But what about someone with a mental disorder? <crickets>

Sadly, people with mood disorders have often not been shown much sympathy. You might have a different skin color, but for centuries bipolar folks were not only stigmatized for being "weird" and marginalized but they were institutionalized. People from every nation have locked them in creepy sanitoriums.

So, might Oxford provide a bit of inspiration for bipolar sufferers today? They come in all ages, genders, and races!

Oxford changes the focus academically, too. Instead of viewing William Shakespeare as racist, sexist, misogynistic, and an imperialist, Oxford might be seen as someone who knew about feeling outcast personally.

Therefore, his plays championed emotional equality for women and people of all races, and because he supported the Essex rebellion, political reform too.

Unfortunately, most Stratfordians think Oxford is just too mommy-dearest creepy.

They will loudly proclaim, "Even if Edward de Vere did experience bipolar disorder, then we should make it Facebook official that Oxford can NOT be the real author. He might have been multi-polar, for all I care, but he could not write the beautiful plays, sonnets, and poetry of the 'real' author." They do not like him. They believe he DID have the frightening appearance of a monster; inhumanly evil or dangerous

But this is crazy talk! It is like saying an African American person cannot be a great writer because of his or her skin color.

Does having bipolar disorder mean that one cannot have talent or success in life? Absolutely not!

In fact, the opposite is true. Many mood issues are often linked to creative people. Do a Google search for mental health and creativity.

Like Adrian Monk, Oxford's bipolar disorder may have had its pros like not being able to sleep may have caused Oxford to read or write more.

Feeling different than others might have led him to research medical remedies found in ancient texts.

After all, could not some of the ancient Greeks and Romans have visited "bipoland" too?

14

Conspiracy Theory

Some people still do NOT believe that the "Deepthroat" individual in the Nixon administration feared for his life.

Or why a person close to Hitler or Pablo Escobar might worry.

Likewise, some people have a tough time swallowing the idea that someone close to Queen Elizabeth I, who knew Greek and Latin but secretly wrote plays, would not want their authorship publicly known. Never mind the fact that playwright Christopher Marlowe had died violently in 1593.

In those days, if someone hated you, they could claim they saw you at church confessing your sins to a Priest.

So, why do people believe that it would be impossible for Stratford to act as a "front man" for another writer without hundreds of people knowing about it? This is not true.

Back in the late 1500s and early 1600s, did every quarto feature the name of the playwright? No. The actors were the rockstars. Many times, the playwright's name was not printed on the title page. Then, after both men were long dead, in 1623, The First Folio was published.

So, prior to the publishing of the First Folio, could someone *pretend* to be a playwright and get away with it? Absolutely.

It is like self-service checkouts. They came out in 2008 and not to brag, but I frequently used to make "mistakes". Nowadays, with all the security cameras and people personally checking receipts before exiting, it is utterly disgusting how few errors I make at the self-service checkout.

What about keeping Oxford's madness a secret? Might Queen Bess have crossed her arms and said in a calm voice, "Oxford may twitch and faint, but he has been very loyal to me. He carried the sword for me when I last visited Scotland, so if I ever hear of his madness spoken in public, heads will roll. Understood, Lord Burghley?" With that in mind, the servants might have politely called Oxford eccentric, strange, or a "weirdo." But never "mad."

This is an actual rendering of Edward de Vere carrying the Chamberlain's sword for Queen Elizabeth I. (Apparently, the artist failed to show that Edward's free hand also carried her big purse.)

My point is this: might the queen have known about his madness but felt compassionate toward Oxford because the misfortune was not his fault?

> In his 2016 article, *Shakespeare and Madness* author, Will Tosh, quotes the French writer Joubert, who wrote: **our first instinct might be to laugh at a man 'who became frenzied or maniacal,' but our laughter must be stifled when 'we think about the great loss of his senses and understanding he has suffered.** Joubert said, **'we experience compassion because of the misery, and more still if this misfortune does not come through his own fault.'**

Remember, Oxford had first come to the royal court at age twelve after his father had died and his mother had quickly remarried. So, Queen Elizabeth had witnessed Oxford's youthful fainting spells firsthand.

If Edward later confided to her that he often wanted to kill himself, what might she have done? The Queen knew his symptoms were not his own fault, and so if she had warned Lord Burghley that she best not ever hear about Oxford's mood disorder what would happen? Would everyone in town know about it? Or would it be kept hush-hush?

As of 2020, not one person has ever commented about Oxford's "madness," have they?

According to the book, *Palladis Tamia* by Francis Meres published in 1598, Meres praised the earl of Oxford. He gave him credit for being "**the best in comedy amongst us.**" But NO plays written by Edward de Vere have ever been found. Why is this?

Did Queen Elizabeth NOT want someone known to be "abnormal" to be writing comedies about her? Nowadays, my wife does not like me to post any pictures of her on Facebook without her prior consent because she thinks I might post a picture that would make her look bad. Can you imagine if I wrote a funny play about her and did not tell her? She would kill me! Could Queen Elizabeth have said something like this to Oxford?

"Write one word about me or my court and I will kill you." Or even worse? "I will have you committed."

If the queen knew Oxford at times seemed moopy, would she have wanted his name attached to any plays? No. Rulers can be fickle people. If she woke up one morning on the wrong side of the bed, his authorship of a play could be turned against him.

Here is some circumstantial evidence for Oxford provided by Alexander Waugh who claims Francis Meres KNEW that Oxford was the "legit" author, but could not publicly say so; and therefore, his book *Palladis Tamia* conveyed a hidden message about Oxford.

We will visit this secret message of Francis Meres later in this book.

Do These Thoughts Resonate?

Writing a play may have made Oxford brim with pride. But what if he got a migraine headache whenever someone stared at him, and then his paranoid personality might have convinced him not to claim the authorship?

Oxford might have dreaded the spotlight. Yet other days, or simultaneously, in a mixed state, he may have wanted the attention! This is a rough example to show how bipolar disorder works.

It also raises the question: how would a well-educated man like Edward de Vere know a fledgling actor who called his home address Warwickshire?

One person who might have known both men was a London printer by the name of Richard Field.

15

Richard Field

Richard Field worked as a printer near Cecil House and did some printing for William Cecil. Like William Shakespeare, Field also hailed from Stratford-upon-Avon.

Field's father worked as a "whittawer" (leather worker), and we recall that John Shakespeare was also called a "whittawer." So, might John have told his son to look up Richard Field when he went to London?

But if this is how Oxford met Shakespeare, through Richard Field, why would Oxford give up his masterpieces to a common boy from Stratford-upon-Avon?

Before I continue, let me pause for just a minute and tell you an Oxford story. After being schlepped over to Cecil House at age 12, Oxford's maternal uncle, Arthur Golding wanted to take the boy's depressed mind off his father's death and his birth mother's absence.

Realizing the boy was an expert in Greek and Latin, Golding asked Oxford to translate the first four books of Ovid's *Metamorphoses*. Can this be proven? No. It is pure speculation.

The only person to publicly comment on this was the poet Ezra Pound, and he did not claim Edward de Vere was responsible for translating the work. Pound simply claimed that Golding's interpretation was the most beautiful book in the whole English language.

He added, *"It's my opinion and I suspect it was Shakespeare's" (Pound 1934, 58).*

In another essay, Ezra Pound claimed: ***"Is there one of us so good at his Latin, and so reading in imagination that Golding will not throw upon his mind shades and glamours inherent in the original text which had for all that escaped him?... it is certain that 'we'...have forgotten our Ovid since Golding went out of print." (Pound 1985, 235).***

Why might we consider a youthful Edward de Vere to be involved in translating Ovid? In writing about Arthur Golding, author John F. Mims found it wonky that Arthur Golding – a Puritan who had spent much of his life translating the religious sermons of John Calvin – would undertake to translate Ovid. Why? Highly religious, Arthur Golding had also translated David's, "***A Book of Psalms.***"

> In 1567, Mims wrote: "He [Ovid] was the darling of a dissolute society and author of a scandalous handbook of seduction... and especially given how much **racier** this translation is than Ovid's original."

Thinking logically, why would a Puritan make his translation racier than the original? Could Oxford as a teenager had translated all fifteen books of Ovid's *Metamorphoses* but gave all the credit to his uncle, Arthur Golding? Could he have done this?

Hold that thought!

If Oxford wrote *Venus and Adonis* as well as *The Rape of Lucrece*, would he give ALL the credit to William Shakespeare? Hold on!

If Oxford wrote thirty-seven plays and 154 sonnets, would he really give ALL the credit to someone else?

Might someone with extreme self-doubts do this? Is it possible? Remember how Oxford's poetry showed that he lacked self-confidence when compared to the "real" author? Is this the reason? Might this be critical to solving our cold case mystery?

I wondered if there was a link between bipolar disorder and self-esteem.

Using Google, I queried, "Studies on bipolar disorder and self-esteem", and if you do this too, you will discover that several studies DO address this topic. Bottomline: most scientists DO believe there is a correlation between bipolar disorder and low self-esteem. The sizes of the studies are low, and though some will state that "more study is advised", researchers have concluded: self-esteem is seen as "a marker" that points to bipolar disorder. One report stated:

"Subjects may experience high self-esteem with mania and low self-esteem with depressive symptoms. But overall: The self-esteem of remitted BD (bipolar disorder) patients is significantly lower than that of normal controls."

So, let us return to the year 1588. His part in the Spanish Armada war disrupted, so Oxford came back home to discover that one month earlier, his wife, Anne Cecil de Vere, had perished after giving birth to their youngest daughter. Oxford's biographer Alan H. Nelson makes it seem like Edward de Vere celebrated his wife's death because he drank heavily, gambled, and had plenty of sex. He also spent money frivolously and lost custody of his children to his wife's family.

But what if Edward was just self-medicating? Did his coping mechanism worsen his mental stability? What if to escape his deep despair, Oxford turned to what he had done as a young boy who had lost his father? What if he had translated Ovid's poem, Venus & Adonis, to help him keep his mind from dwelling on his wife's death, and how he had treated her? It is possible. It makes sense and it fits the timeline from when the poem was written 1589-1591.

Also, Oxford would not have to worry about his nosy, Puritan uncle looking over his shoulder. This time, he could produce his own racier version. Once finished, what would he do with Venus & Adonis? He did not write it for money.

Enter Richard Field. Field's print shop was located close to Cecil House. In fact, Field had printed some pamphlets for William Cecil (also known as Lord Burghley) who was Oxford's foster-father and father-in-law.

William Cecil was also Henry Wriothesley's legal guardian. Rather than let Oxford toss the poem into the trash bin in 1591, perhaps Field suggested that Oxford should pay him to publish the poem. They could do so under a pseudonym.

Richard Field had grown up in Stratford-upon-Avon and knew of a man three years younger than him with a funny last name. The man's wife had recently given birth to twins and was hard up for money. And he was loyal. Why not print the poem under the name William Shakespeare and dedicate it to Henry Wriothesley?"

It is important to remember that at that same time, 17-year-old Henry Wriothesley was living at Cecil House along with Oxford's 14-year-old daughter, Elizabeth Vere.

William Cecil was trying to get the very wealthy Henry Wriothesley to marry his granddaughter, Oxford's daughter, Elizabeth Vere.

What if Edward de Vere did not want his daughter to marry him?

If William Cecil did not allow Elizabeth to receive Edward Vere's letters to her, what could her father do? Would a father be able to write a message of "don't marry my daughter" in a poem called *Venus & Adonis*? At the end of that poem, Adonis does gets killed by a wild boar – and a wild boar can be found on the de Vere family crest. (see the picture below)

More importantly, with the publishing of these two poems began the Oxford/Shakespeare connection. Here was a way for Edward de Vere to get his works performed in public without risking getting in trouble for being an anonymous author.

Do These Thoughts Resonate?

If you believe Shakespeare read forty books to write two poems that he dedicated to Henry Wriothesley to win his patronage, wouldn't you expect Henry Wriothesley to write a "thank you note" back to William?

In 1590, Henry Wriothesley was under the age of twenty-one and was not legally allowed to offer a patronage to any writer. At least, not without William Cecil's approval because Cecil was his guardian. So, the tale about William Shakespeare writing *Venus and Adonis* to seek a patronage from Henry Wriothesley? It is pure speculation.

Moving along, do people in love also act a little crazy? Definitely on TikTok, but 400+ years ago people also talked about being "lovesick."

Does the "real" author talk about lovesickness in any of the plays? We will look at lovesickness in just a bit. But what about the Sonnets? Can bipolar symptoms be found in the "real" author's sonnets? We will find out, in the next chapter!

16

The Sonnets

The prima facie case for Stratford states that because Stratford's name can be found on the First Folio, The Sonnets and the long poems, then he must have written the plays, poems, and sonnets. This makes sense, doesn't it?

The following is an excerpt from a poem by Victoria Lucas from a book of poetry published in 1963.

I am silver and exact.
I have no preconceptions.
Whatever I see I swallow immediately
Just as it is,
unmisted by love or dislike.
I am not cruel, only truthful,
The eye of a little god, four-cornered.
Most of the time I meditate on the opposite wall.
It is pink, with speckles.
I have looked at it so long
I think it is part of my heart.
But it flickers.
Faces and darkness
separate us over and over.

Who was the author of this poem? Easy, the name on the cover states Victoria Lucas, so we know that she authored this book.

But were you aware that a version published in the United States in 1970 shows a different author's name? This book cover shows the poems were penned by Sylvia Plath.

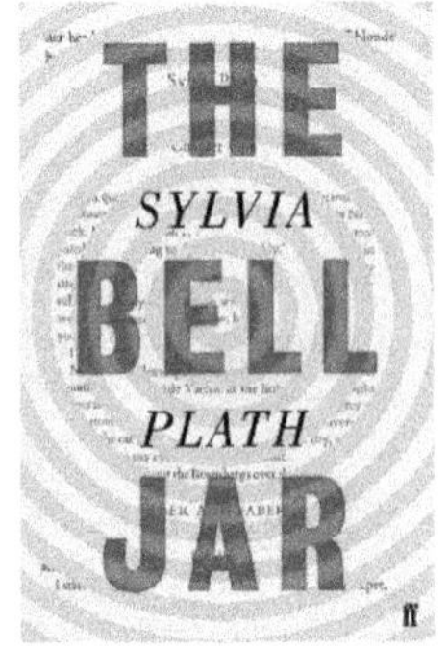

Victoria Lucas was her *pen name.* Similarly, on Twitter, many people use "fake Twitter handles" to hide their true identities. Or what about when someone is involved in "Catfishing"? This is where a person will create a fictional persona or fake identity on a social networking service to target a specific victim.

Might William Shakespeare also be a pseudonym? If so, how would we know?

I suggest we use bipolar disorder symptoms as a guide.

Let us check out the poem below, and just for kicks, see if you can discover any indications of bipolar disorder in it. What are we looking for? Symptoms like self-pity, despair, lack of energy and low self-worth.

When, in disgrace with fortune and men's eyes,
I all alone beweep my outcast state,
And trouble deaf heaven with my bootless cries,
And look upon myself and curse my fate,
Wishing me like to one more rich in hope,
Featured like him, like him with friends possessed,
Desiring this man's art and that man's scope,
With what I most enjoy contented least.
Yet in these thoughts myself almost despising,
Haply I think on thee, and then my state,
(Like to the lark at break of day arising
From sullen earth) sings hymns at heaven's gate.
For thy sweet love remembered such wealth brings
That then I scorn to change my state with kings.

Notice how the writer's mood changes? He moves from feelings of pessimism and a dark, deep, depression to an almost manic state of happiness!

One minute he is "cursing his fate", despising himself and basically shopping for a noose when suddenly, he is, as my mother used to say, "as happy as a lark."

Were you aware that someone with a bipolar personality, like Edward de Vere, occupies the polar extremes of despair and ecstasy? Most of us are like Switzerland. We inhabit the middle ground and generally feel contentment. In Sonnet 45, he writes

"Sinks down to death, oppressed with melancholy."

Read that again. Oppressed means cruel, unfair or needlessly controlling. An adult who locks a child in a room is oppressing the child. Do not these words "sinks down to death, oppressed with melancholy" sound almost suicidal?

Viewing the sonnets with an eye toward bipolar depression, can you see how William Shakespeare relates love and madness?

We notice this in Sonnet 147 when he writes:

> Desire is death, which physic did except.
> Past cure I am, now reason is past care,
> And frantic-mad with evermore unrest.
> My thoughts and my discourse as madmen's are,
> At random from the truth vainly expressed:
> For I have sworn thee fair, and thought thee bright,
> Who art as black as hell, as dark as night.

William apparently gave someone his heart, but she ghosted him. Man, that sucks, but instead of moving on, like yours truly would, his thoughts become "frantic-mad" and "evermore unrest."

He cannot believe she dumped him. Me? Adios. No problem. I get it. But not him! He cannot sleep and goes mad. Just listen to him:

> How can I then return in happy light?
> That am debarred the benefit of rest
> When day's oppression is not eased by night
> But day by night and night by day oppressed
> And each though enemies to either's reign
> Do in consent shake hands to torture me.

Insomnia is another symptom of bipolar disorder and so is a feeling of depression, which can be found in Sonnets 33, 34, 36, 37, 43, 44, 49, 50, 61, 62, 66, 71, 72 and 74.

So is talking about death which is found in forty-one sonnets.

Adding them up, over 36% of the 154 sonnets explore feelings of *depression*, *death*, and *insomnia*.

These are the same things Edward de Vere complained about in his real life, but William Shakespeare? In his real life, William never mentioned them.

Today scientists believe depression and creativity go hand in hand. A link to a study of creativity and bipolar disorder can be found at the back of this eBook. But know there are several famous writers like Edgar Allen Poe and Kurt Vonnegut who endured depression.

Finally, two men are credited with bringing the sonnet form to England from Italy: Sir Thomas Wyatt and Henry Howard, earl of Surrey.

Henry Howard *was the uncle* of Edward de Vere. This might explain how Oxford would know how to write a sonnet.

But what about Stratford? <crickets>

Did you know there are also several crazy coincidences between Oxford's real life and the plays of William Shakespeare?

A rumor began circulating during the reign of England's Queen Elizabeth the first that she was having a love affair with Edward de Vere, the 17th earl of Oxford, and that she had a child by him who was being raised as the third Earl of Southampton. One historian of the Elizabethan era who reported this rumor dismissed it as "wildly improbable"; many scholars over the past four centuries have scoffed at it. The image of the Virgin Queen, so carefully cultivated by Elizabeth for political reasons, still maintains a powerful grip on the imagination, even though new evidence has come to life that she had at least three children, possibly more.

from ***The Secret Love Story in Shakespeare's Sonnets*** by Helen H Gordon

17

"Mad" Real Life Events

My mother-in-law's name was Clemencia de Palomo, but she never used the "de" in her name. It was always just Clemencia Palomo. Similarly, if Oxford lived in Los Angeles today, I think he might ditch the "de" and rebrand himself as Edward Vere.

I mention this because Edward Vere pronounced his last name like "ever" and in the play, *All's Well that Ends Well*, the word "ever" is used twenty-seven times. Interesting, isn't it? Like a subconscious reveal. "Ever" = E Vere.

In real life, Queen Elizabeth had ordered Oxford to be locked in the Tower of London for impregnating a lover who had a "dark" complexion. Her name was Anne Vavasour.

She, her baby, and Edward de Vere were locked up in the same jail cell. One night, William Cecil arranged for his daughter, Anne Cecil – Oxford's real-life wife – to exchange places with Vavasour and the baby. Then, in the dark, unknowingly, Oxford made love to his wife!

Anne Vavasour

In the morning, the two reconciled their marriage like the happy-ending tale of Bertram and Helen in the Shakespeare play, *All's Well that Ends Well*.

Do you really believe that he *unknowingly* made love to his wife? I don't. <insert sarcasm here> Like he did not know the baby was gone and a different woman had entered the bed. This from the man who always complains he cannot sleep? In any case, this example shows how writers will often color a work of art by drawing on their life experiences. But what about Macbeth? Did someone need to kill a man to write this play? No. Instead, Stratford could have used his imagination. But truth is often stranger than fiction.

At seventeen years of age, Edward de Vere DID kill an unarmed man. He was practicing sword-fighting and stabbed an under-cook who belonged to Burghley's household staff.

The cook, Thomas Brinknell, bled out and died, but with Lord Burghley's help, the death was later ruled a "suicide." So, Edward Vere may have gotten away with murder.

However, the suicide meant the cook could NOT be buried on church grounds, and it caused the cook's wife and her children to have to beg for food in London.

What if Edward imagined he saw her later in his life, or ACTUALLY saw her? Perhaps he wrote *Macbeth* to talk about his own inner demons concerning madness and murder. Remember that feelings of guilt and paranoia are symptoms of bipolar disorder and are sometimes labeled "agitated depression?"

Agitated depression is not a medical term, but some people use it to describe this feeling of anxiety and depression. It is a mixture that often involves anger and restlessness and then afterward feelings of regret, guilt, and paranoia.

In *Macbeth*, Act III scene 4, for example, Macbeth sees Banquo's ghost when no one else can. Why? Macbeth is mad. Paranoia and a belief in magic are evidence of his madness, and Macbeth's murders of Banquo and Duncan display a certain knowledge of a paranoid schizophrenic insanity which causes Macbeth to mumble aloud and have guilty hallucinations.

People can say "this is sheer speculation" that Oxford is talking about his own personal demons in *Macbeth;* but then, do not writers write about what they know? Can Macbeth be an allegory about the good and evil that exist in all men, and about our struggle with these two sides of our bipolar personality?

Here is another example of madness. This comes from the play *Twelfth Night*. Could the events from this play have happened to Edward de Vere when he was a child?

My masters are you mad? Or what are you? Have you no wit, manners, nor honesty, but to gabble like tinkers at this time of night? (Twelfth Night II. iii.)

In this scene from Twelfth Night, Malvolio admonishes Sir Toby and Sir Andrew for being drunk and rowdy. He even goes as far as to suggest that their rough behavior and total disregard for others could be a sign of madness. Malvolio's attitude becomes significant as later in the play, Sir Toby enacts his revenge on Malvolio by making him appear to be mad in Olivia's company.

Madness here is seen as "fun and wild behavior" and includes anything that falls outside the bounds of "proper" behavior.

"Sir Tobias never was a man thus wronged. Good Sir Tobias do not think I am mad. They have laid me here in this hideous darkness." (Twelfth Night IV. ii.)

Again, Malvolio speaks about madness as being normal. This time, Malvolio has been imprisoned as a madman and we laugh. But to exploit the joke even further, Sir Toby pressures Feste to dress up as a priest and perform a mock exorcism on Malvolio. The reference to darkness helps to punctuate the theme of madness as play. There is the physical darkness of the prison itself, but darkness offers a figurative allusion to madness. It is a state of confusion.

Therefore, Malvolio is not the only one who is mad (as he rightly points out), but those around him are too. Everything has been turned upside down and civility has been pushed aside so that everyone can freely indulge in craziness.

But in real life, darkness must have frightened 8-year-old Edward de Vere because he broke all the windows inside his dorm bedroom when he had attended Queens College.

"2s 4p. from March Expenses," Allan H. Nelson writes, "These payments were for the repair of window-glass which might have been broken from the inside or the outside. Either way, the young lord's presence spelled trouble for the college."

The school charged the boy 2 shillings 4 pence to buy new window glass, but why would an 8-year-old behave like this?

Had he been placed in a dark room, whipped, and left there alone? With no electricity or candles, how might he bring light into the room? Answer: break the windows.

I am as mad as he, if sad and merry madness equal be. (Twelfth Night III. iv.)

In these lines, Shakespeare seems to suggest that Olivia is as mad as Malvolio, who has been acting weird after reading Maria's letter.

However, Olivia's "madness" functions as an expression of her deep love for Cesario – a love that he does not return. He has plunged her into a state of "deep melancholy" or depression. Her madness stems from her state of lovesickness, while Malvolio's is a merry kind, and originates from his over-inflated optimism. He believes Lady Olivia really DOES love him.

Twelfth Night links the theme of madness to wild behavior and lovesickness. Love, Shakespeare seems to say, has the power to inhibit rational decision-making and some people who are called "mad" are just normal love-crazed people.

But let us not forget about darkness. Because don't mad people harbor dark thoughts too? A full-blown metaphor of darkness can be found in *Othello*. Here, Shakespeare writes from the perspective of the jealous "dark-skinned" Moor. We know that while he was away in Italy for 16 months, Oxford's wife had given birth to a daughter but instead of being happy, Oxford became overwhelmed with feelings of anger and jealousy.

He bitterly believed in her infidelity. Upon his return, the earl gaslighted his wife and disowned the child believing he had been made a cuckold.

According to author Alan H. Nelson, Oxford verbally and mentally abused his wife for five years. Around this time, Oxford's cousin accused him of atheism, fornication, drunkenness, gambling, and pederasty. (Pederasty meant same-sex attraction, not child molesting.)

Not to excuse Oxford's bad behavior, but do not these behaviors fit untreated bipolar disorder?

What about "depressive" symptoms? Do they show up in the Bard's works?

Obviously, Jacques from *As You Like It* comes to mind because he was always a "melancholy" person.

But here is the thing: in 18 of 37 plays written by William Shakespeare or in 48% of them – there is talk of someone feeling "melancholic" or depressed. Why?

Isn't there usually some hidden Freudian correlation between an author's written words and the person thinking the words?

Might the author be subconsciously talking about himself?

Oxford had three daughters and in the play *King Lear*, the author tells us how people who lose their sanity are not just reckless or foolish. In Lear's case, madness is beyond his control. He wants to be normal but cannot help himself. In this case, the cause of his madness might be due to Lear's advanced age.

In Act 1, for example, we see Lear's slow decline into madness. His sane moments are prominent, and at first, he seems foolish rather than mad, but as the act progresses his sanity slowly dims, and his rash judgments cannot be blamed on foolishness. By the end of Act 1, it appears evident that Lear is going mad. Especially when he banishes Kent for being honest.

Kent: *Kill thy physician and thy fee bestow upon the foul disease. Revoke thy gift, or, whilst I can vent clamor from my throat, I will tell thee thou dost evil.*

Lear: *Hear me, recreant! On thine allegiance, hear me! That thou hast sought to make us break our vows, which we durst never yet, and with strained pride to come betwixt our sentence and our power, which nor our nature nor our place can bear, our potency made good, take thy reward.! (KL Act 1, Scene 1, 165-181)*

Are Lear's speeches of madness describing Oxford's own lack of proper judgment, blindness to the truth, impulsive decisions, and incredible mood swings?

Lear shows himself to be unpredictable, unfair, and impulsive. By the end of Act I, Lear realizes that he is going mad, and begs to himself and the Gods to prevent this from happening.

Lear: *O, let me not be mad, not mad, sweet heaven! Keep me in temper; I would not be mad! (KL Act 1, Scene 5, 44-45)*

Coming up, we shall connect more dots with the real author and bipolar disorder, but we will also address the claims of those who believe that Oxford can NOT be the *real* author because *he died* in 1604.

If some of the plays were written after 1604, it would be *impossible* for Edward de Vere to be the "real" author, wouldn't it?

18

1604 and Mr. Monk

Stratfordians love to joke, "RIP Edward de Vere, you would have enjoyed the plays of William Shakespeare." In other words, if any of the plays were written after 1604 then Oxford could not be the "real" author because dead men cannot write plays.

In this chapter, we will view three objections to Oxford's authorship and see how Mr. Monk might have responded to them.

Objection# 1: Oxford died in June 1604 If several of the great plays were written after 1604, then Oxford can NOT be the real author. However, Mr. Monk might claim, "Dating the plays is a fool's errand because they could have all been written prior to 1604 and revised a few years later by someone else."

Mr. Monk has a point. How would we know today if someone changed a few lines after 1604? Could not someone have added a line or two about the Gunpowder Act or the Bermudas?

Sylvia Plath died in 1963. Yet, nineteen years later, in 1982, who won the Pulitzer Prize for poetry? Sylvia Plath. She won for her book of "Collected Poems."

Did Sylvia Plath author any new poems after she died in 1963? No. They were all written before. Plus, Sylvia Plath left written instructions to her family not to put her name as the author of *The Bell Jar.* She was embarrassed about her poems not being good enough.

Oxford died in 1604. But what if 19 years later in 1623, his thirty-six plays were collected and published under his pseudonym: William Shakespeare.

What if Ed Vere had left written instructions that his real name not be attached to any of the plays? In Oxford's case, could not his works have been revised and edited by someone after 1604? Or could Sir Francis Bacon have been involved? Yes.

Why Francis Bacon?

Sir Francis Bacon

Edward de Vere's childhood guardians were William Cecil and his wife Mildred. She was the sister of Sir Francis Bacon's mother, so Sir Francis *was an uncle* to Oxford's daughters.

If they had asked Uncle Francis to help get their father's works ready to be printed, would he have refused them? Probably not, as they were his nieces. Does this mean Frances Bacon was the original author of the plays? No.

Objection #2: Didn't Shakespeare plagiarize Thomas North?

Recently, there has been a lot of ink spilled about how William Shakespeare plagiarized the plays of the English translator, Sir Thomas North, who had translated *Plutarch's Lives* from a French author.

Dennis McCarthy and Michael Blanding deserve credit for advancing the idea that William Shakespeare rewrote several of North's old plays in their book, *North by Shakespeare*.

But Mr. Monk might say, "None of North's source plays have ever been found. **Plus, what if North and Oxford had found the same ancient source material?** Oxford was an expert in Latin so would not the two translations by North and Oxford be the same or similar?"

However, McCarthy and Blanding do show how several speeches, word-for-word, are found in *Julius Caesar, Timon of Athens, Coriolanus,* and *Anthony & Cleopatra:* all they claim come from the work originally written by Sir Thomas North.

Who knows? Oxford may have plagiarized North. Or not. North may have left a copy of his works at Fisher's Folly, where Edward de Vere could have easily read them.

During the early 1580's, Sir Thomas North, Robert Greene, Lyly, Lodge, Marlowe, Nash, and Peele would gather at a house called "Fisher's Folly" to write historic dramas to support the queen's war effort. Who owned Fisher's Folly? **Edward de Vere**. Did Sir Thomas North attend these meetings? Yes.

So, is it possible that North may have left a copy of his book, *Dial of Princes* behind and needing paper, might Oxford have used it to scribble down lines for an actor? Absolutely. Christopher Marlowe lived at Fisher's Folly making Oxford his proprietor. What was William Shakespeare's connection to Christopher Marlowe? He had none

However, Thomas North made a living translating classical books from Spanish and French, and *Plutarch's Lives of the Noble Greeks and Latins* was originally written in Greek, translated to Latin, then French, then English. Did you know it was common for tutors to require their students to translate both the Greek and Latin versions? Both Greek and Latin versions of *Plutarch's Lives* are listed as part of the library of Sir Thomas Smith, Oxford's boyhood tutor.

There is a receipt showing that Oxford purchased the French version of *Plutarch's Lives* before leaving for Italy, so does it not make sense that he intimately knew *Plutarch's Lives*?

Interestingly, several of the men featured in *Plutarch's Lives* suffered from epilepsy such as Pythagoras, Hannibal, Socrates, Plato, Alexander the Great, Julius Caesar and Dante. If Oxford read the book three times in three different languages he must have worshipped the epileptic heroes in it.

Oxfordian Stephanie Hopkins-Hughes goes even further than a fan-boy fascination. (www.politicworm.com)

She believes Thomas North may have asked Oxford to edit *Plutarch's Lives* for him because North's first translated book, *The Dial of Princes,* was NOT critically well-received. Some scholars even accused North of plagiarizing an earlier Spanish translation of the book. But if Oxford had rewritten *Plutarch's Lives* for North and then penned the two dedications of the book for North, how would we know today?

According to Ms. Hughes look for the word "love" in North's written words because the word "love" was something often used by Oxford but not North. For example, the "To the Reader" excerpt found in *Plutarch's Lives* reads:

> "Now, for the author, I will not deny but **love** may deceive me, for I must needs **love** him with whom I have taken so much pain, but I believe I might be bold to affirm that he hath written the profitablest story of all authors."
>
> The dedication to Queen Elizabeth goes: "There is none (your highness best knows) that teacheth so much honor, **love**, obedience, reverence, zeal, devotion to Princes, as these lives of Plutarch do."

Did you notice the word "Englished"? The title of the book reads, Plutarch's Lives **Englished** by Sir Thomas North. I believe this was the first time Englished was used like this, and it is something Shakespeare liked to do – create a verb out of a noun.

What do Opponents of Edward de Vere Say?

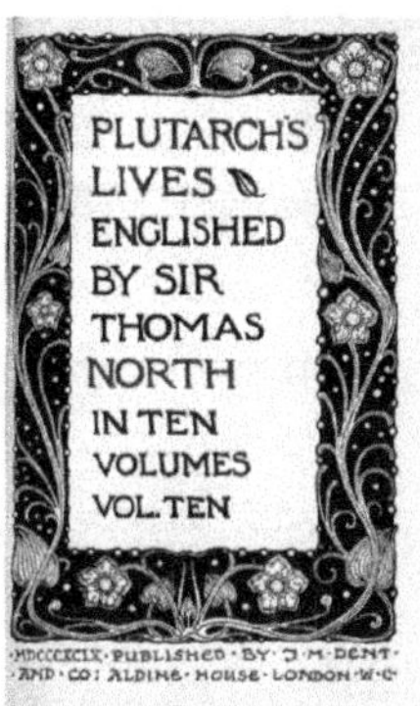

Some folks claim that Thomas North did not like Oxford, so he would *never* ask him to translate *Plutarch's Lives.* But during the "Spanish Armada years", any ill will between writers was put on the backburner. Playwrights were needed to support the war effort.

Objection #3: Were not Shakespeare's plays a collective effort?

Some of the history plays may well have been a collaborative effort, but they still required someone to make the final "director's cut." Oxford makes sense because he had studied Greek as a child. Why else do we find so many instances of *suicide*?

In *Romeo & Juliet,* for example, Romeo and Juliet commit suicide. In *Hamlet,* there are nine deaths and at least two confirmed suicides. What happens to Brutus and Cassius in *Julius Caesar*? They both kill themselves. Othello? He commits suicide after murdering his love with a dagger. The play, *Anthony and Cleopatra*? It ends with five suicides, including the ones by Anthony and Cleopatra. Plus, want to guess how the poem, "*The Rape of Lucrece*" ends? She commits suicide. So, would a collective group of writers *prefer suicides* to happy endings?

In Elizabethan times, suicide was considered a mortal sin and a crime against the crown. However, to the ancient Greeks, suicide was viewed as acceptable when it was "performed in the right circumstances," or "rationally justified" and "to escape the shame of defeat and surrender."

But was this concept taught in grammar schools? No. Not to beat a dead horse, but are not thoughts of suicide also a symptom of bipolar disorder? Yes.

When we add all the fainting, madness, and suicides in the plays, along with expressing feelings of despair, depression and insomnia in the sonnets, the results point to a classically educated individual who experienced depression often. Not a vagabond actor from Stratford, or a group of crazy people.

19

Connecting the Dots

As an English major at UCLA, I once had a class where my assignment was to write a paper on the theme of love in Sonnet 116. This happened to be my instructor's favorite sonnet, and if the number 116 does not ring a bell, the poem starts out like this, "*Let me not to the marriage of true minds admit impediments*."

I probably should not have been drinking when I penned this essay. I wrote that when it came to love poems, this one sucked! In fact, I believed that I could make an even better one by rewriting a few lines. So, I did, and I included my newly minted sonnet in my paper. I truly felt confident about it too! Believe it or not, this is a true story.

The day we got our essays back, the professor had prepared a pop quiz. While taking the test, I can recall her sashaying around the classroom returning papers, one by one. There were about 30 students in the class, and my heart pounded loudly in my ears when she plopped my 4-page masterpiece on my desk.

Normally, a letter grade would be clearly visible on the first page, but on mine, there was nothing. No grade. I flipped through all the pages to see if she had written any remarks, and there, on the last page, she had written this sinister message: "Robert, please see me after class is over, in my office."

This could not be good. It is like when your girlfriend says, "we need to talk." You know she is NOT going to talk about football or anything fun, right?

When I got there, the door to my instructor's private office was open, so I entered, shut the door behind me and sat down. She took off her glasses, gazed at me and said, "Robert, I have been teaching Shakespeare for over 20 years now and I have read a lot of papers on this sonnet, but I have never read one quite like this. Your observations are different than the "ideal" love we spoke about in class, but I do admire your courage. I think the world needs more original voices." She then asked me for my paper. I gave it back to her, and she scribbled an "A" on it. You could have knocked me over with a feather.

Now I know that this sounds braggy as hell so let me share with you how I had rewritten Sonnet 116 and a simple observation I had made. Will you agree? Or will you *completely* disagree with my professor? If so, it would not be the first time in my life this has happened. See, to some folks, Shakespeare is like Texas, and you should NEVER mess with Texas. Here is the original Sonnet 116 by William Shakespeare.

Let me not to the marriage of true minds
Admit impediments. Love is not love
Which alters when it alteration finds,
Or bends with the remover to remove.
O no! it is an ever-fixed mark
That looks on tempests and is never shaken;
It is the star to every wand'ring bark,
Whose worth's unknown, although his height be taken.
Love's not Time's fool, though rosy lips and cheeks
Within his bending sickle's compass come;
Love alters not with his brief hours and weeks,
But bears it out even to the edge of doom.
If this be error and upon me prov'd,
I never writ, nor no man ever lov'd.

Now, if you have ever been in love, does this sonnet really ring true? If so, it did NOT ring true to me. Maybe it was because I was 19 years old and I had recently broken up with my girlfriend of 7 months who had cheated on me, but at that moment in time, to me, the writer had blown it. He had failed to mention one acutely important word which is why I had felt so strongly about rewriting his sonnet. I honestly believed my version was better with it. Here is Sonnet 116 rewritten by me:

> Let me not to the marriage of true minds
> Admit impediments. Love is not love
> which alters when its alteration finds
> Or bends with the remover to remove.
> Oh no, it is an ever-fixed mark
> that looks on tempests and is never shaken
> It is the star to every wandering bark
> whose worth's unknown, although his height be taken
> Love involves trust, like how I trust you, but,
> Trust is hard to gain and easy to lose.
> Love alters not with his brief hours and weeks
> But bears it out to the edge of doom.
> Love means caring for someone no matter what
> For love may be blind, but *never* is trust.

You probably noticed how I added the extra lines about trust, right? So, what do you think? Is it not true? For example, if a woman *swears* that she loves you but then she cheats on you, will her words still ring true to you? No. Might you still have feelings for her? Yes. But if you have experienced the emptiness, betrayal, and manipulation of being cheated on – does it matter if she keeps telling you how much she loves you? No. Therefore, isn't having someone you can trust important when you are in love?

FAST FORWARD to present day. The question I want to ask you is this: is it possible the "real" author had trust issues? Did he fear opening up to someone else? What if he had a phobia? Or what if he felt like he could *never* trust someone? I wanted to know how he used the word "trust" in his other works.

Steve Jobs once said we can only connect the dots by looking backward. And, because some people might think, well, what if William just knew someone who fainted? I want to help you to understand the correlation of the "real" author to bipolar disorder (BD) by looking backward and pointing out three traits that scientists say are *unique* to people suffering from bipolar disorder. They are empathy, time, and trust.

20

BD Trait#1: Trust

In his plays, the real author uses the word "trust" 183 times. But because of mistaken identities in the plays, what he often says is "do *not* trust me or anyone else for that matter." For example, in *All's Well that Ends Well*, he writes, *"Love all, trust a few and do wrong to none."* By the way, if you are a student and want to know how many times a word was used by Shakespeare in his plays, please visit: www.shakespeareswords.com

Ok, back to trust. If you trust but a few, then you will protect yourself from getting hurt. In *Much Ado About Nothing*, we hear, *"Let every eye negotiate for itself/And trust no agent, for beauty is a witch."*

Summarizing this play, he seems to say that deceiving someone is not truly evil because deception is something that can be used for either good or bad.

In Sonnet 23, the speaker seems unable to deal with his trust issues because he loves but "fears to trust." He writes:

As an unperfect actor on the stage,
Who with his fear is put beside his part?
Or some fierce thing replete with too much rage,
Whose strength's abundance weakens his own heart.
So, I, for fear of trust, forget to say
The perfect ceremony of love's rite,

And in mine own love's strength seem to decay,
O'ercharged with burthen of mine own love's might.

Here scholars say, the speaker is like someone with stage fright. He is tongue-tied and cannot say the things he wants to because his love is so strong. But I disagree.

Does it not seem like he is saying, "I do not feel secure about myself because my moods are so brutally unpredictable?" First, he is "replete with too much rage" and then later, "over-charged" with love.

Doesn't it sound like the results of his online BD test might read: "Consistent with bipolar disorder. Please seek treatment."

The line, "So, I, for fear of trust" means, "Because I do not trust myself." Think about it.

Finally, in Sonnet 138, the speaker expects *dishonesty*. He writes:

When my love swears that she is made of truth,
I do believe her, though I know she lies,
That she might think me some untutored youth,
Unlearned in the world's false subtleties.
Thus, vainly thinking that she thinks me young,
Although she knows my days are past the best,
Simply I credit her false-speaking tongue:
On both sides thus is simple truth suppressed.
But wherefore say she not she is unjust?
And wherefore say not I that I am old?
Oh, love's best habit is in seeming trust,
And age in love loves not to have years told.
Therefore, I lie with her and she with me,
And in our faults by lies we flattered be.

The line, "Oh, love's best habit is in 'seeming' trust," implies that the truth does not matter when someone is in love. But that is effin' crazy, isn't it?

Trust is the foundation of love. Without trust, you have nothing. Do you think most women would go along with a guy who pretends to trust? Some yes. But the speaker seems content with building a relationship on lies and dishonesty. Yet, most relationships that lack trust tend to self-destruct; don't you agree?

Do lies and deception match the beliefs of the man from Stratford? No. Stratford's father, John Shakespeare, may have been viewed as a crook because he had often appeared before the magistrates in London and had done some crooked and illegal wool dealings. Not William.

William Shakespeare was intent on clearing his family's name from the disgrace of being evicted from William Clopton's farm.

William Shakespeare purchased a coat of arms. He borrowed money with others to purchase commercial real estate. He rubbed elbows with King James I. He left money to buy mourning rings, so no person would ever dare to call him a crook after he died. Nobody.

William Shakespeare was a gentleman who could be trusted because he paid all his debts and then some. His father may have had trust issues; but not him.

In fact, when William Shakespeare acquired the 107 acres from John Combe for £320 in May of 1602, he failed to attend the closing. (It WAS mandatory back then).

So, the court steward claimed the property would remain in the hands of the owner until the new purchaser came forward to receive it. Why didn't William come forward? Because he *trusted* Combe.

Stratford did the same thing when he purchased property from Walter Getley in September of 1602; this was for a cottage on Walkers Street, otherwise known as Dead Lane, in Stratford-upon-Avon.

The Folger says: "Walter Getley performed his role, but Shakespeare was not there officially to take possession." Why not? Stratford trusted people.

But what about Edward de Vere? After his wife's passing, did Oxford's father-in-law trust him to raise his daughters? No.

Did Queen Elizabeth trust de Vere to oversee any important military post? No.

Did Oxford's first wife Anne Cecil trust him? No.

Did Oxford trust his wife, Anne? No.

Did Lord Burghley trust Oxford with any property? Or was he concerned that Oxford might just sell it and squander the money on shoes? You know the answer.

Did Oxford even trust himself?

In her article, *Narrative Selves, Relations of Trust and Bipolar Disorder*, author Nancy Nyquist Potter writes,

"The bipolar patient may [also] be coping with delusions, general cognitive problems, and severe mood swings. Marked shifts in mood and activity can diminish others' trust in the patient as well, thus, both self-trust and trustworthiness are undermined. **The illness, not the patient's character is the cause."**

Let me rephrase that last line: *The illness* causes the trust issue, not the person's character. That brings us to trait number two: time.

21

BD Trait# 2: Time

The next unique bipolar trait has to do with time. Here are the two lines I deleted from Sonnet 116 because they referred to time:

Love's not Time's fool, though rosy lips, and cheeks Within his bending sickle's compass come.

Most experts claim that here the speaker talks about "an everlasting love", but to me it seems a little creepy. Notice how the "real" author envisions time as holding a sickle?

Doesn't that make you think of the figure of Death, holding a scythe? Like the Grim Reaper? If so, doesn't that make his love seem possessive? Ever watch the TV show Dateline? If so, you will often hear some killer say, "If I could not have Gloria, then no one else could either!"

This is called a "pathological" love, or one bordering on obsession. Like the song, "Every Breath You Take" by Sting. He will always be watching her. But is that healthy? No. Then I asked myself: might this be the way a person experiencing symptoms of BD views time? Perhaps "Love is not Time's fool" means time can play tricks on us. Time can age flowers and people ruining their beauty, but not my love. My love will endure forever, and it will never die. Interestingly, like the issue of trust, researchers claim time is an essential feature of bipolar disorder.

An article in *Schizophrenia Bulletin* from 2018 states: *"Time is an essential feature of bipolar disorder. Manic and depressed bipolar disorder patients perceive the speed of time as either too fast or too slow."*

When a manic episode of BD happens, for example, time plays a trick and moves quickly. We view this in *Love's Labor's Lost* when King Navarre says, "*Now at the latest minute of the hour/Grant us your loves*" to which Princess of France answers: *"A time, methinks, too short to make a world-without-end bargain in."* (LLL V2 782-3).

Doesn't it seem like King Navarre's version of time is arrogant? Because the King feels happy, we all should smile and fall in love instantly! Time is perceived like the adage, "Time flies when you are having fun." For this reason, many bipolar people are guilty of not wanting to sleep. They want to keep "clinking glasses and shaking asses."

But time can play another trick. When someone experiences a depressive episode, time can appear to move so slowly it can feel like a burden. In Richard II we hear "I wasted time and now Time doth waste me."

In Sonnet 60, the real author writes: "Like as waves make towards the pebbled shore, so do our minutes hasten to their end." Each minute slowly dies a small death. In Sonnet 77, the "real" author writes, "Thou by thy dial's (or sundial) shady stealth may'st know, /Time's thievish progress to eternity."

Time is like a bandit that can slow life down and drag it on without end.

This slower, unhappy concept of time can be seen in the writings of Sylvia Plath, who was diagnosed with bipolar disorder after her death. Did you know, Sylvia Plath's father died when she was young, and then her mother became inattentive to her? (In Oxford's case, his father died, and his mother remarried. But in Plath's case, her mother had to go to work.) Sylvia got married but when her spouse cheated on her, she authored poems about feeling depressed and suicidal.

I mention Sylvia Plath because some people will tell me "You are not a doctor. You cannot diagnose a person *after their death* with bipolar disorder. It is pure speculation and dangerous!"

However, more than a decade after her death, physicians DID identify Sylvia Plath with having Bipolar II affective disorder. And I get it.

Doctors diagnosed her – not an armchair detective like me. But should a caregiver who notices hyperactive behavior in a child mention it to the child's parents? Or only if the caregiver has a medical license?

By the way, did medical doctors truly know how to treat or diagnose people with BD in the 1580's? No. So, could not a poet who wrote sonnets almost 400 years earlier have also endured bipolar disorder? Here is Plath's sonnet, called *To Time.*

> Today we move in jade and cease with garnet
> Amid the ticking jeweled clocks that mark
> Our years. Death comes in a casual steel car,
> Yet we vaunt our days in neon and scorn the dark.
> But outside the diabolic steel of this
> Most plastic-windowed city, I can hear
> The lone wind raving in the gutter,
> his Voice crying exclusion in my ear.
> So, cry for the pagan girl left picking olives
> Beside a sunblue sea, and mourn the flagon
> Raised to toast a thousand kings, for all gives
> Sorrow; weep for the legendary dragon.
> Time is a great machine of iron bars
> That drains eternally the milk of stars.

Like William Shakespeare, Sylvia Plath sees time as something that sadly affects people's lives. Time moves fast or slow, depending upon how one is feeling but continually drains and drains and drains everything – even "the milk" or the life of stars.

Did William Shakespeare of Stratford-upon-Avon personally share this view? No. Stratford *carefully planned* for things. Gilly wrote his own epitaph in advance, along with a last will and testament. Besides gifting Anne Hathaway his 'second-hand' bed, he thought to include money for his daughters and mourning rings for his trusted friends, remember?

Shakespeare's attitude towards time was forward-thinking because he prepared for matters in advance. He had his lawyer draft a will months before his death because one should be prepared for the unknown.

Who knows? One late-night, binge-drinking bender could lead to meeting sleep's cousin, death.

Before talking about BD Trait #3, empathy, it is important to relay a conversation I had with one Stratfordian on why he believes William Shakespeare DID write the works of Shakespeare. What are the two things that convince him?

22

Speech Headings

Some scholars claim that there are "contemporary references" too many to count to prove Shakespeare wrote Shakespeare. This makes it seem like hundreds of people who were William's contemporaries wrote about him. However, to scholars contemporary references means "a list of books with William Shakespeare's name as author." For example five versions of the same quarto with Shakespeare's name on it. Or one titled *King Lier* and others *King Lear*. These are all considered "contemporary references", but do they prove anything? No.

Similarly, we are told stage directions and character names found in the speech headings of some of the old quartos prove an "authorship by committee" rather than an authorship by one person. But is this evidence or just conjecture?

Many scholars point to the old quartos where names of certain actors were handwritten in, instead of the real character's name(s). Therefore, instead of "Enter Falstaff" the character in the play, the stage direction reads, "Enter Kemp."

William Kemp was an actor with the earl of Leicester's Servants and The Lord Chamberlain's Men. So, if Kemp or "Kempe" was written in the stage directions and on some of the speech headings, then does this prove Kemp wrote his own lines? Sorry, but that is a hard "NO" from me. It might prove that someone could not recall Falstaff's name but that's about it.

They also point to the fact that William Shakespeare worked as an actor, and Edward de Vere did not. Oxford was just a rich earl. Not being an actor means Oxford would have had NO experience in writing and directing plays.

But in the year 1580, a letter written by Dr John Hatcher, of Cambridge University, claimed:

... the Heads of the University object to the Earl of Oxford's players showing their cunning in certain plays already practiced by them before the Queen's Majesty the like having been denied to the Earl of Leicester's Servants.

This shows that Edward de Vere's players had already performed his plays before Queen Elizabeth, an honor that had been denied to the earl of Leicester's players.

It also proves that Edward de Vere was not only apparently writing, directing, and acting in plays before the Queen in 1580, but he would travel to do so too.

But changing the speech headings for an actor? Sorry, but like "contemporary references" they are both all smoke and mirrors, signifying nothing.

The last distinctive trait linking the real author to bipolar disorder concerns empathy.

Contemporary Reference Examples

1598 (From Francis Meres's Palladis Tamia: Wits Treasury;
registered September 7)
"Shakespeare"
"Shakespeare"
"Shakespeare"
"Shakespeare"
"Shakespeare"
"Shakespeare"
"Shakespeare"
"Shakespeare"
"Shakespeare"
(printed) (EKC II, 193)
1598 (Title page, Q2 of Richard the Third)
"William Shake-speare"
(printed by Thomas Creede for Andrew Wise) (EKC I, 294)
1598 (Title page, Q1 of Love's Labour's Lost)
"W. Shakespere"
(printed by William White for Cuthbert Burby) (EKC I, 331)
1598 (Title page, Q2 of Richard the Second)
"William Shake-speare"
(printed by Valentine Simmes for Andrew Wise) (EKC I, 348)
1598 (Title page, Q3 of Richard the Second)
"William Shake-speare"

Above is a list of "contemporary resources" that even shows William Shake-speare on the title page of *Richard II*.

23

BD Trait#3: Empathy

The last distinctive trait linking the real author to bipolar disorder concerns empathy. Empathy is defined as the ability to understand and share the feelings of others. Some scholars have claimed that many of the female roles found in the canon are so strong and well-written that NO man could have penned them. For this reason, it has been suggested that a woman may have authored the Shakespeare canon because women tend to be much more empathetic. This led me to wonder, what are three traits of empathetic people? Here are the ones I came up with:

1. People with empathy are curious. They like to reach out to total strangers.
2. Empathetic people often feel concern for those who are being discriminated against.
3. Empathetic folks will "step into the shoes" of other people and show extra concern when tragedies occur.

So, was Stratford known for his empathy? No. We know William Shakespeare did not write letters to his own family, much less reach out to strangers to better understand them, did he? Did he ever travel to any other country outside of England? No. Did he feel concern for women or others who might have been discriminated against? No.

Was he extra-concerned about his wife after they buried their eleven-year-old son? The official church records show that his son, Hamnet was buried on August 11, 1596. About two months later, the official court records show that on October 20, 1596, Stratford paid for a coat of arms.

So, did William Shakespeare spend extra time with his wife or did he rush off after the death of his only son to buy a coat of arms? If so, is that being very empathetic? No.

What about Edward de Vere? Did Oxford like to read and travel? Yes. He generously supported other writers and translators. Did he step into the shoes of others and show extra concern over tragedies? Yes and no.

See, Oxford had a raging temper. People sometimes walked on eggshells around him. His temper was called "violent," which often matches bipolar affective disorder II, and his biographer Alan H. Nelson called him "monstrous" because he was so impulsive, intense, erratic, and explosive. If asked a simple question, Oxford might react with irrational anger and/or lash out for no logical reason.

Some people claim Edward de Vere was a raging psychopath who cared only about himself and that he was the exact *opposite* of an empathetic person. Would not such a lack of empathy disqualify him?

Please realize, bipolar disorder is a MOOD disorder characterized by *opposite* symptoms. The mechanism of what causes these moods to shift back and forth and why is still unknown. So, having a dual identity does not preclude him.

Why? Because someone with BD can have a mood shift and turn from North Pole angry to South Pole happy. Again, it is the nature of the illness, not the character of the person. Also, a recent study involving people with bipolar II affective disorder, showed that some patients have what scientists call extreme empathy. Extreme empathy is an intense, excessive compassion and understanding for others. It can differ from person to person and from day to day.

Could Oxford behave with extreme empathy one day and then act like an angry dick the next? Yes. What proof do we have? Well, the fact that he did manage to spend seventy million dollars in less than a ten-year span should be proof enough.

Also, Oxford was documented by many writers to be unduly generous and giving. Over thirty authors praised and wrote dedications to the earl in their books, thanking him. So, there is proof to Oxford's excessively generous nature and support of the arts. It is not hearsay.

Might someone with bipolar disorder involving extreme empathy explain how the "real" author was able to "step into the shoes" of his female characters? It might also explain how a white male could write about Othello's insecurity as a Black man.

Edward de Vere had visited Italy and lived there for over one year. Might he have cultivated friendships with Jews and Moors while living there? While living in Italy, no one really knew him, so it might have been fun to meet an Italian woman and have her describe her female friends over pillow talk. Is this why the strong women characters refuse to kowtow to men in the Shakespeare canon? Is this why there is a Black man in love with a white woman in *Othello*?

Also, in the plays *As You Like It, Two Gentlemen of Verona, Twelfth Night, Merchant of Venice,* and *Cymbeline* there are many instances of mistaken identity where male actors posed as female characters. The genius of Shakespeare hits us as we watch these plays because sitting in the audience, we feel for these characters and cringe as someone falls in love with someone else who does not reciprocate their affections.

Because male actors played female parts in the plays, his extreme empathy helps to push the theme of gender equality too, doesn't it? But does gender equality match the personality of Stratford? William Shakespeare was a man who bequeathed money for his daughter Judith, but in his will, he dictated various conditions attached with the gift.

What about the fact that Shakespeare's youngest daughter signed her name with a mark indicating that she did not know how to read or write? She will never be able to read her father's poems, plays or sonnets.

Edward de Vere, the 17th earl of Oxford

The Ashbourne Portrait by Marcus Ghheeraedts

http://www.shakespearefellowship.org/Ashbourne.htm

> "The goals of personalized medicine for many disease states are to improve upon past trial-and-error strategies and optimize therapeutic outcomes for patients. In psychiatric diseases such as bipolar disorder, where the risk of suicide is extremely high, achieving these goals is crucial to maintaining patient safety. Although a range of therapies are used for bipolar disorder, supporting evidence is limited, efficacy is low and varies significantly from patient to patient, and adverse effects and potential harms are many."

--- Linda Peckel, "*A Slow Road to Personalized Bipolar Treatment*" in Psychiatry Advisor Feb 2, 2018

24

What Bipolar II Disorder Feels Like

To give you a better idea of what it feels like to endure bipolar mood disorder, here are the words of a woman who talks about living with Bipolar II Disorder (pronounced "bipolar two"). These are her "manic" or "hypomanic" symptoms:

> "I could remember talking so much and so fast that others did not understand what I was saying. They told me to slow down. I could remember times when I felt incredibly brilliant and "greater" than everyone else. All these were clear signs of hypomania, but they were not clear enough to my psychiatrist. He did not get to the bottom of either my severe depression or my symptoms of hypomania. Although, to be fair, bipolar disorder was not his specialty and back in 1998, Bipolar type II Disorder—which contains the presence of hypomania — was not readily understood."

The following are the "depressive" symptoms of another bipolar woman:

> "I was wishing for death every day, could barely get out of bed, and had turned to self-harm for some small measure of relief. I had no idea why these things were happening to me as nothing notable had preceded them, but they were obviously happening brutally."

I do not claim to know what it's like to have bipolar disorder, epilepsy, or both. In my attempt to bring attention to Shakespeare's words and BD, I may have spoken clumsily or with insensitivity. To those readers with bipolar disorder, I apologize. In this book, I have tried my best **not** to use the word "suffer", such as he or she "suffers" from BD. People with bipolar disorder **endure a lifelong condition that creates unusual mood changes,** and they learn to deal with its symptoms. It's not something like the flu that goes away after a few days.

There is a saying among BD bearers that goes: "Bipolar people do not fake feeling depressed. **They fake being okay.**"

So, if a woman experiencing bipolar disorder were in a slump, wishing for death every day in 1998, when medical science had some knowledge about bipolar disorder, what would it be like for a person living in the late 1500's with NO knowledge of bipolar disorder? No meds? And no one to talk to?

Might this explain why the author of the plays speaks about insomnia, dual identities, suicides, fainting and depression in his sonnets?

Is it possible that the real author may have endured bipolar disorder?

25

Almost Final Thoughts

The world has changed since the "real" William Shakespeare lived, and people have made strides in discussing mental health issues in a more open and accepting way. Patients who are diagnosed as being bipolar depressive will NOT be whipped and sent to a dark room but treated with medications such as Lithium, Caplyta, and Latuda.

While psychologists do believe diet and genetics play a role in mood disorders, it is now understood that losing a parental figure at an early age through death or divorce can be a major contributing factor to mood disorders. Over 21% of US adults experience some form of mood disorder in their life. We know Oxford found himself a broken-hearted orphan by age fourteen. Also, besides "mummy" or putting patients in a "dark room", what other treatments were there for people in Elizabethan times who exhibited signs of BD?

Interestingly, one cure can be found in the advice given by writer Kurt Vonnegut. Did you know that the American author Kurt Vonnegut also endured bipolar depression? It is true. So did his son Mark and Kurt's mother. Vonnegut once wrote

> "a writer is lucky because he cures himself every day with his work."

A writer can help alleviate his depression, not by staying in bed, but by bravely getting up every day and writing. Even if it is only writing about things happening in his or her life.

Using the prima facie evidence makes sense. The person listed as the author usually is the author and Stratford seems like a normal enough guy. The Folger proves that William Shakespeare sued a man for £6 ($2,400 in 2020), purchased 107 acres and wrote a horrible epitaph for himself. He sounds like someone today who might commute to downtown Los Angeles.

Did Shakespeare ever once publicly utter aloud about feeling miserable? No. We hear he was convivial. Witty. Ben Jonson described him as "gentle." (Not that many bipolar people are not gentle.) But when left untreated, many people with Bipolar II disorder often have phobias, become fearful, paranoid and have self-esteem issues.

Even those with incredible talent can lose everything without proper guidance and medicine. But having this mental disorder does not necessarily mean a person cannot have talent or success in life.

Please allow me to mention some other famous people who may have displayed symptoms of bipolar disorder but became better-known for their talents. You may recognize a name or two:

Brittany Spears
Winston Churchill
Mariah Carey
Carrie Fisher
Bebe Rexha
Mel Gibson
Demi Lovato
Russell Brand
Brian Wilson
Jimi Hendrix
Ernest Hemmingway
Catherine Zeta Jones

Frank Sinatra

If Kurt Vonnegut, who passed away in 2007, told people that writing down his feelings "cured" his bipolar issues, why couldn't it have worked for a writer who was known for writing 'the best comedies' at Queen Elizabeth's court in the late 1500's?

Might this help to explain why the *real* author wrote over one million words? Like a shark needs to keep moving to stay alive, he needed to write to survive. My hope is that you might be inspired by this book to do more research into the issue of bipolar disorder. Perhaps you might know of someone who is experiencing the symptoms but have not realized that the symptoms are part of a more significant problem.

You might even be motivated to lend that person a hand.

If you DO happen to bump into a student, teacher, or human with bipolar disorder, please support them for being who they are.

And realize that this disease does NOT define someone. It is just a part of who that person is.

So, if you are experiencing bipolar disorder and there is no one available to talk to, write down your feelings.

Who knows? You might be the next "William Shakespeare" or "Kurt Vonnegut!"

Helpful Resources

- National Suicide Prevention Lifeline: **(800) 273-TALK** (8255); available en Español,
- 1-888-628-9454; Chat, Lifeline Crisis Chat Program. emotional distress.
- Crisis Text Line: Text HELLO to 741741.
- This is a free and confidential health hotline open 24 hours a day. crisis.
- Boys Town National Hotline: (800) 448-3000; Text VOICE to 20121. facing a crisis.
-

26

Conclusion

When I was a boy, the Wicked Witch of the West from the movie *The Wizard of Oz* scared my sisters. That witch gave them nightmares. Not me. No siree. But the flying monkeys? I swear, those damn monkeys scared the crap out of me! But after thinking about it, I told my brother that the ending sucked. I mean, why would anyone leave a bucket of water on the kitchen floor? Wouldn't you be afraid that a flying monkey (or two) might get mad, pick up the bucket, and douse you? My brother claimed I ruined the entire movie for him.

Likewise, some people believe that I have ruined William Shakespeare for them. They want to believe a local boy wrote the works. Educators have taught us that a mountain of proof exists, so why would they want to trick us? The story of a boy genius offers hope that someone smart could be born in a lower class and whip "a rich snob" and who doesn't like that story? But when we view the mountain of evidence online, like the proof for Flying Monkeys, it does not exist.

Nowadays forensic science can be used to clear suspects and exonerate persons mistakenly accused or convicted of crimes. Although no biological DNA evidence remains after 400 years, traces of a rare mood disorder do still exist in the words of William Shakespeare. The fainting and "mumia" indicates epilepsy which may have led to bipolar disorder for the person who wrote the canon. Are these symptoms a match to the reckless spending, despair, and other characteristic actions of Edward de Vere as recorded by historians? If so, then our DNA-like match might be added to our other pieces of circumstantial evidence. However, if asked to name a suspect, what might Mr. Monk say?

"**Follow the money!**" So let us wrap us our cold case mystery by starting there.

The British Museum claims that 750 copies of the First Folio were originally published in 1623, and back then, paper was outrageously expensive. It has been estimated that the cost to print 750 copies would have run about $550,000 in today's money.

The book was dedicated to two multi-millionaires. The "two fine brethren" William Herbert and Phillip Herbert were brothers who had close ties to Edward de Vere's family. Not William Shakespeare's.

Phillip Herbert *was married* to Susan de Vere, *the daughter* of Edward de Vere. Her sister, Bridget de Vere had been engaged to William Herbert, but their engagement had been called off.

Most of us have heard the adage about the "happy wife leading to a happy life." So, did Philip Herbert publish his father-in-law's plays under his penname William Shakespeare to keep his wife Susan happy?

This married man raises his hand in agreement.

But what happens when we follow the money with William Shakespeare in mind?

Following the Money with Stratford

A bronze memorial in England honors two actors: John Heminges and Henry Condell. These two men allegedly collected his old quartos (that had ever been performed) and brought them to a publisher to be made into the First Folio. They did this "without ambition of self-profit or fame, only to keep the memory of so worthy a friend and fellow alive."

This story never made sense to me. Why? It implies that William Shakespeare's wife never wondered about how her vagabond spouse made enough money to purchase pricey real estate.

I have been married for over 25 years, and I swear my wife can sniff out every dollar I make. But Shakespeare's wife? Even though she lived in the second biggest house in town, she never figured out how her husband raked in so much cash.

Instead, two selfless actors brought his 36 plays to a publisher. Not her. For this reason, no bronze statue exists for Shakespeare's clueless wife.

These two actors claimed they had collected all the old quartos from the Kings Men that had been performed and brought them to the publisher. Most people have heard this story before and just go along with it. But stop and think.

Twenty of the plays had NOT ever been performed in public, and in 1613, the Globe Theater burned to the ground. Isn't that where the old quartos would have been kept?

More Reasons to Suspect Edward de Vere?

Fourteen years older than William Shakespeare, Edward Vere wrote poetry as a youth that was published in the book *Paradise of Dainty Devices*. If a boy genius from Stratford-upon-Avon had written poetry as a child, wouldn't someone have noticed it?

Oxford received an extensive Latin education, studied law, and had books at his fingertips. He grew up in a mansion like the White House and had attended college when he was only eight years old. Are not most children who attend college at an early age thought of as a genius?

Oxford also traveled. He went to Scotland. (MacBeth) Lived in Italy. He saw people dying. He also had on staff two secretaries John Lyly and Anthony Munday who likely kept copies of all his written work.

After Oxford's death, they might have given all his plays and sonnets to his widow.

The plays and sonnets would have been passed on to her step-daughters upon her death. We know that Oxford's widow died in 1609, and in 1609 the sonnets by William Shakespeare were first published. What if the de Vere daughters had brought them to a publisher after their stepmother's death? It would have been embarrassing for William Shakespeare because the dedication spoke about our "ever-living poet," and he was still alive!

Oxford's daughters may have learned from that experience too because Shakespeare's wife, Anne Hathaway died on August 6, 1623. Then the First Folio was registered two months later on November 8, 1623. Or is this just a coincidence?

Today people in the mafia might call William Shakespeare a "stand-up guy." Even if he were tortured, he would refuse to talk.

How many letters to people did he write? Zero, which means he kept his big mouth shut. He may have been incredibly brave, stupid, ignorant, or poor, but we should all appreciate him nonetheless because he may have risked his life.

If it was not for Gilly and his bravery, we might not today have the Shakespeare canon.

So, for that we should all be grateful. In addition, doing so may have also saved Oxford's oldest daughter.

Helen H Gordon author of *The Secret Love Story in Shakespeare's Sonnets* along with Hank Whittemore, author of *The Monument* have offered an intriguing theory about why de Vere may have written the two forgotten poems.

They claim Oxford and Queen Elizabeth were once lovers, and she gave birth to a son named Henry Wriothesley. Therefore, Oxford may NOT have wanted his daughter to marry Wriothesley, because he was her own **stepbrother**. But how could he get through to warn her? Elizabeth Vere and Henry Wriothesley both lived at Cecil House, where her grandfather, William Cecil would be intercepting all messages sent to them. Cecil wanted the arranged marriage to go through at all costs. So, what could Oxford do?

Elizabeth Vere

He wrote something Cecil could not seize. Oxford penned two long poems under a pseudonym, William Shakespeare and then dedicated them to the young Henry Wriothesley. His plan worked too because Henry *declined* the marriage arrangement to Elizabeth Vere.

But can it be proven today that William Shakespeare got paid to use his name? No.

At least not directly. In the year 1600, for example, William Shakespeare sued John Clayton in a court of law. William claimed that in 1592, he had loaned Clayton £7 and he had never been repaid. A judge agreed and awarded William Shakespeare the sum of £10.

What does this judgment prove?

According to the judge in 1600, Clayton DID borrow the money from Shakespeare but where would Stratford get £7 to lend to a stranger in 1592? Remember, in 1592, William Shakespeare was flat broke and without a trade.

Experts tell us William allegedly wrote *Venus & Adonis* and dedicated it to Henry Wriothesley because he needed the money. He wrote two 'forgotten' poems to gain a patronage from a rich, earl and for this reason, he dedicated the poems to him.

But Wriothesley was born in October 1573 so in 1592, he would have been only 19 years old and under the legal age to sign a contract. (Ms. Gordon believes he was conceived on January 6th, also known as *Twelfth Night*.)

And, in over 400+ years, nothing has been found written by Henry Wriothesley to verify that William Shakespeare ever received a patronage from him. It is pure speculation that has been taught as "fact."

Venus & Adonis was printed in April 1593, and back then it took about one year to do the typesetting. Is it not possible that William Shakespeare could have received a boatload of money from a generous earl, desperate to stop his daughter's arranged marriage?

Does this explain why William had the extra money to lend to John Clayton? Does this make sense to you?

Hearing this, Stratfordians will usually offer the old Obi Wan Kenobi excuse and say, "Sorry, but this is the **wrong** Shakespeare. You see, according to the text of the Shakespeare lawsuit, the loan was transacted on May 22, 1592, in the parish of St. Mary le Bow in London. The Bard hailed from Stratford-upon-Avon, so this is NOT the William Shakespeare you are looking for."

But do not Stratfordians also claim William Shakespeare left his tiny hamlet for London in 1587? Yes, and the John Clayton lawsuit puts William Shakespeare smack-dab in London in 1592.

In addition, the "real" William Shakespeare was known to sue people for lesser amounts of money. In 1608, for example, he sued to recover a debt **of £6** from John Addenbrooke.

So, if a judge back in 1600 awarded £10 to Shakespeare and ruled Stratford HAD lent Clayton the money, who should we believe? Modern Stratford experts? Or a judge who oversaw the evidence back in 1600? (I am putting my money on the judge!)

These days many scholars scoff at the use of ciphers and secret messages, but in a world where Catholic priests performing the act of Confession were seen as traitors to be gutted before they were hanged, does not secrecy make sense?

Remember how earlier I had mentioned that a secret message could be found in Francis Mere's book, *Palladis Tamia*? According to Alexander Waugh, if the last (or worst) English writer in a list of **seventeen** writers is paired with the last (or worst) **seventeen** classic writers, the result reveals a different order. Wasn't Edward de Vere the **17**[th] earl of Oxford?

For an interesting and engaging video presentation on this topic, please visit Alexander Waugh's YouTube channel.

Edward Earl of Oxford	
Menander	Doctor Gager
Aristophanes	Master Rowley
Eupolis Atheniensis	Master Edwards
Alexis Terius	John Lyly
Nicostratus	Lodge
Amipsias Atheniensis	Gascoigne
Anaxandrides Rhodius	Greene
Aristonymus	**Shakespeare**
Archippus Atheniensis	Thomas Nash
Callias Atheniensis	Thomas Heywood
Plautus,	Anthony Munday
Terence	Chapman
Naevius	Porter
Sext. Turpilius	Wilson
Licinius Imbrex	Hathway
Virgilius Romanus	Henry Chettle

Reversing the order, we can see that Shakespeare is paired with **Aristonymus** while the G.O.A.T. (greatest of all time) writer becomes Edward de Vere, the earl of Oxford.

Edward de Vere's first tutor Sir Thomas Smith wrote *De Repubica Anglorum* and in this book, Smith pleaded to stop torture by rack or rope.

Sir Thomas Smith knew about this subject firsthand because he had personally acted as a "rack-master" for King Henry VIII. Thomas Smith knew well the rack, the manacles and the "scavenger's daughter": all tools used for racking, disemboweling, and other cruelties. Might Sir Thomas Smith have planted a seed in young Edward de Vere's head about the consequences of writing negatively about a ruler? It is not a stretch to think so. (Bad pun intended)

The authorship question reminds me of an optical illusion. Have you ever seen the one titled 'the old woman/ young woman'? When first viewed, many people will insist they can only see an older woman but after a while, if you look hard enough, you may discover that a younger woman flanks her shoulder.

The old woman never authored any poems as a child and grew up in a town called "densely illiterate" by Mark Twain. Meanwhile a young woman has looked away in plain sight for over four hundred years. Waiting. Forgotten. Neglected. Hopefully, this little book has helped to bring her to your attention. (The chin of the young woman acts as the nose of the old woman.)

Edward de Vere died in June 1604, and later that same year, his daughter, Susan de Vere, got married. During that Christmas holiday season in 1604, seven Shakespeare plays were performed at various mansions. Many Oxfordians believe this was a special nod to Oxford.

But no public mourning happened after Shakespeare's death.

Who was the real author of the Shakespeare canon?

Some claim the author was Sir Francis Bacon. Others believe it was Christopher Marlowe. Or even William Shakespeare of Stratford-upon-Avon.

But the percentage of people who fainted often and then wrote about epilepsy as well as "mumia" a drug to cure epilepsy was small. The percentage of those people today who boast having *both* epilepsy and bipolar disorder is even smaller. Estimates vary, but studies show this rare combination affects less than 0.05% of the entire population on earth so it is *like a genetic fingerprint* or DNA. Edward de Vere exhibited symptoms of bipolar disorder during his lifetime. These symptoms were like those experienced by the writer of the Shakespeare canon.

Yet some people will say that studies suggest that forensic DNA analysis is only 95% accurate so it could be wrong. Just like people tell me that to identify someone by a mental illness is speculative. Only qualified doctors can diagnose these patients and even then, their diagnosis may be flawed. Yet these same people are unbothered using websites to screen patients for bipolar disorder symptoms. Go figure.

Learning about Edward de Vere, we discover a flawed human who had his own demons, struggles, and a brutal world when he lived. We learn not only about people, places, and events of the past, but about the adversities Oxford overcame, and this knowledge helps us connect as people too.

Over twenty years ago, I got a call from the vice-president of a bookselling chain. Tasked with finding a new location for their company, I was surprised that the spot he liked best was only two-doors down from a large Barnes & Noble bookstore.

"Aren't you concerned about the competition?" I asked him. "Nah. We find that when customers already know of one place where they can buy books, and we are almost next door, they will check out our store more easily. It offers customers a second choice. Fast-food chains like McDonalds and Taco Bell do this all the time."

Likewise, Edward de Vere originally wrote the Shakespeare canon, but his plays, poems and sonnets would not be here today without the special pairing of the Stratford commoner. This combination has been famously credited solely to William Shakespeare but like Scooby Doo & Shaggy, or Batman & Robin or Woody and Buzz Lightyear, what we know today as the works of William Shakespeare would not exist without the energy, imagination, and melancholy of the 17th earl of Oxford, Edward de Vere. He stamped the Shakespeare canon with his heart and soul. It is time to acknowledge and honor him.

I would also like to recognize the Folger Shakespeare Museum and the many fine Shakespeare scholars like Sir Stanley Wells, Paul Edmondson and Allan H. Nelson whose works I have drawn on and without them this book could not have been written. Credit also goes out to the many great Oxford scholars too like Hank Whittemore, Stephanie

Hopkins-Hughes, Bonner Miller Cutting, Alexander Waugh and many others, even those critical of my work have helped me.

Queen Elizabeth may have been fierce, ferocious, fickle and paranoid, but she was NOT a stupid person. According to Sir Stanley Wells the play *Richard II* was authored in 1595. Isn't it possible that she may have seen the play when it first came out? So, most likely, the king's resignation scene **had been added later** which would have infuriated her.

Therefore, viewing the play in 1601, Queen Elizabeth would have known who wrote *Richard II* and who had added the scene because she had viewed the play before, so why would she need to execute a man with a penis-punned name?

Instead, the sights, sounds and smells of a man drawn and quartered would be enough to ensure no future performances of the play would happen again during her lifetime. Nor did the queen need to imprison Edward de Vere. Queen Elizabeth had treated him like a son from age 12, so she would never kill him. Instead of a life sentence in the Tower, might she see that Edward de Vere's 'real' punishment be that he never be allowed to receive credit as the "real" author of his works of genius? Would not this penalize him more than anything else?

I will leave that for you to decide.

See, there was a method to my madness!

Remember to keep in mind what Ben Jonson had advised back in 1623, "Reader, look Not on his Picture, but his Book."

Ben Jonson

Lastly, I want to thank **you** for spending your valuable time with me! If this book helps one student meet with a counselor or health care professional regarding mental health issues, then it was well worth writing. The lesson is this: "Depression is not your fault. You are not your illness, and it makes sense to reach out to a doctor for help. Do not be afraid. It is normal to do so."

So, that is it folks! With a bit of luck, I will see you around the bend. Or maybe I will catch you on social media. You might even see me taking out my trash on a Friday morning!

If this book resonated with you and you would like to leave your thoughts of it in the form of an online review, that would be appreciated. But if not, that is fine too.

And if you feel I have been insensitive to people living with bipolar disorder, I truly apologize as that was not my intent.

Or as one great philosopher once said, "Why is that person giving me half of a peace sign? Weird."

I love you, thanks again and take care!

Robert Boog

(P.S. Want to continue your journey down this 400+ year old rabbit hole? Check out the website of Hank Whittemore at https://hankwhittemore.com/. Visit: the List of Links & Sources at the back of this book for more resources.)

List of Links & Sources

1. [1]https://www.historic-uk.com/

   [2] Shakespeare, A Study of Facts and Problems EK Chambers, 1930

   ^ E.A.J. Honnigmann, 'Shakespeare's Life' in 'The Cambridge Companion to Shakespeare' edited by Margeta de Grazia and Stanley Wells, Cambridge: Cambridge University Press, 2001, pp 1-12, pg. 5
2. ^ https://sites.google.com/a/pvlearners.net/elizabethan-education/home/grammar-schools
3. ^ Mabillard, Amanda. *Shakespeare of Stratford: Shakespeare's Siblings. Shakespeare Online*. 12 Sept. 2000.
4. ^ https://www.bl.uk/collection-items/ovids-metamorphoses [The British Library]
5. ^ *Imagining Shakespeare's Wife: the afterlife of Anne Hathaway, Sheil Katherine West,*
6. ^ Faints, fits, and fatalities from emotion in Shakespeare's characters: survey of the canon Kenneth W Heaton BMJ. 2006 Dec 23; 333(7582): 1335–1338. doi: 10.1136/bmj.39045.690556.AE
7. ^ See Citations page regarding Blackfriars Gatehouse on page 133 of this book
8. ^ NELSON, A. (2003). Youth: 1562–1571. In Monstrous Adversary: The Life of Edward de Vere, 17th Earl of Oxford (pp. 34-67). Liverpool University Press. Retrieved November 27, 2020, from http://www.jstor.org/stable/j.ctt5vjkcp.9
9. ^ May, Steven W., et al. "The Poems of Edward DeVere, Seventeenth Earl of Oxford and of Robert Devereux, Second Earl of Essex." *Studies in Philology*, vol. 77, no. 5, 1980, pp. 1–132.*JSTOR*, www.jstor.org/stable/4174058.
10. ^ NELSON, A. (2003). Italy: 1563–1562. In Monstrous Adversary: The Life of Edward de Vere, 17th Earl of Oxford (pp. 7-33). Liverpool University Press.
11. ^ https://www.bl.uk/shakespeare/articles/shakespeare-and-madness,
12. ^ Ogburn Jr., Charlton. The Mysterious William Shakespeare. McLean, VA: EPM Publications, 1984.

13. ^ *Mania and Low Self-Esteem.* By Winters, Ken C., Neale, John M. Journal of Abnormal Psychology, Vol 94(3), Aug 1985, 282-290
14. ^ NELSON, A. (2003). Youth: 1562–1571. In *Monstrous Adversary: The Life of Edward de Vere, 17th Earl of Oxford* (pp. 34-67). Liverpool University Press.
15. ^ https://politicworm.com/tag/edward-de-vere/page/2/
16. ^ Griffin, Miriam. "Philosophy, Cato, and Roman Suicide: II." *Greece & Rome*, vol. 33, no. 2, 1986, pp. 192–202. *JSTOR*, www.jstor.org/stable/643257.
17. ^*Narrative Selves, Relations of Trust and Bipolar Disorder, Potter Nancy Nyquist* Johns Hopkins University Press,Volume 20, Number 1, March 2013, pp. 57-65
18. ^ https://academic.oup.com/schizophreniabulletin/article/44/1/54/3835420
19. ^ Jackson, Macd. P. "Stage Directions and Speech Headings in Act 1 of Titus Andronicus Q (1594): Shakespeare or Peele?" *Studies in Bibliography*, vol. 49, 1996, pp. 134–148. *JSTOR*, www.jstor.org/stable/40372032. 12 Feb 2021
20. ^ Mabillard, Amanda. *William Kempe.* Shakespeare Online. 21 Feb. 2021. http://www.shakespeare-online.com/biography/willkempe.html
21. ^ Benazzi, Franco. "Major Depressive Disorder with Anger: A Bipolar Spectrum Disorder?" *Psychotherapy and Psychosomatics*, vol. 72, no. 6, 2003, pp. 300–306. *JSTOR*, www.jstor.org/stable/48510104. Accessed 11 Jan. 2021.
22. ^ Jones, James T. R. "Walking the Tightrope of Bipolar Disorder: The Secret Life of a Law Professor." *Journal of Legal Education*, vol. 57, no. 3, 2007, pp. 349–374. *JSTOR*, www.jstor.org/stable/42894032. Accessed 18 Mar. 2021.
23. ^ https://neuro.psychiatryonline.org/doi/full/10.1176/jnp.2009.21.1.59
24. ^ Honigmann, E. A. J. "HOW HAPPY WAS SHAKESPEARE WITH THE PRINTED VERSIONS OF HIS PLAYS?" *The Modern Language Review*, vol. 105, no. 4, 2010, pp. 937–951. *JSTOR*, www.jstor.org/stable/25801484.
25. ^ Previously in 1619 when he was hoping to win the contract to print what became the First Folio, William Jaggard began wooing Susan Herbert and her husband with the dedication to *Archaio-Ploutos* (the book employs many of the same typographical devices which appeared four years later in the Shakespeare Folio):To the most Noble and Twin pair of truly honorable and complete perfection: Sir Philip Herbert... earl of Montgomery...As also the truly vertuous and noble countess his wife, the lady Susan, daughter to the Right Honourable Edward Vere, earle of Oxenford..."[8]
26. ^ https://deveresociety.co.uk/wp-content/uploads/2015/12/NL_2020_27_2_April_FINAL_05Apr2020-JS.pdf p 32
27. ^ https://deveresociety.co.uk/wp-content/uploads/2015/12/Hess-SOF-Summer-2018.pdf

28. SCHWARTZ, MURRAY M., and CHRISTOPHER BOLLAS. "The Absence at the Center: Sylvia Plath and Suicide." *Criticism*, vol. 18, no. 2, 1976, pp. 147–172. *JSTOR*, www.jstor.org/stable/23100084.
29. Sanazaro, Leonard. "THE TRANSFIGURING SELF: SYLVIA PLATH, A RECONSIDERATION." The Centennial Review, vol. 27, no. 1, 1983, pp. 62–74. JSTOR, www.jstor.org/stable/23739384. Accessed 11 Nov. 2020.
30. Sylvia Plath, *The Collected Poems*, (New York, Harper & Row Publishers, 1987)

About the Author

Robert "Bob" Boog is a real estate broker who lives with his wife Roxana and three dogs in Santa Clarita, Ca. The father of two sons, Brandon Boog and Kevin Boog, Bob is a graduate of UCLA with a BA in English, and claims he writes for fun. His books include: Hang Shakespeare, **Is She 'The One'?**, **The Real Estate Rookie** and **My Real Estate Nightmare**: *based on a true story which means it happened more or less like this but with uglier people.*

Robert also narrates some of his books on ***Audible.com.***

Robert's songs can be found on YouTube, Spotify and Apple or at www.robert-boog.com.

https://www.youtube.com/channel/UCXg4eIkf0Z-fuGXyNiaMbtQ

Index

www.ingramcontent.com/pod-product-compliance
Lightning Source LLC
Chambersburg PA
CBHW070627310726
48982CB00001B/191
* 9 7 8 1 7 3 6 5 1 2 1 2 8 *